HENRIETTA'S EYEFUL:
The missionary
and the bouncing bottom

By

Guy Shackle

 New Generation **Publishing**

For Mary Koemtzopoulou

Chapter 1

As villages go, this one should have gone long ago. Off the face of the earth. Anywhere. This was the firm opinion of Henrietta Tobias. And she did hold very firm ones. As missionaries do. Especially when shaken to the core by a most ghastly sight.

She had returned from her work in the steaming jungles of Africa for a rest. To rebuild her strength before going back into the fray.

She was tall and thin, with her greying hair pulled back in a bun. She had a long nose that was always busy. It started twitching the moment she arrived in Hatchett and never stopped. Nothing escaped her.

She had followed the family tradition. Her great grandfather had preached on what was then called the dark continent. He had been speared by one of his congregation while reciting the Lord's Prayer. As it was a Sunday, he was roasted over a fire for lunch rather than boiled in a pot. His harrowing demise shocked his descendant into becoming a vegan. Then a craving for a really full fat cheese turned her into a vegetarian. She was then undone by a lamb chop a careless waiter brought by mistake. But those were the only concessions she ever made.

Hatchett was the best and oldest kind of English village. Traditional to its boot heels. A pretty place with whitewashed thatched cottages and trim hedges. Honeysuckle and roses entwined themselves round its doorways. It had a civilised air. Just right to regain one's energy in. Or so Henrietta thought.

There was a catholic convent on one edge of it and a protestant church on the other. There was a post office, a pub, a little restaurant and a red bricked bungalow for the local constable. On top of the hill stood the big house occupied by a retired colonel.

The missionary arrived on the first day of spring. This was not recognised in Hatchett by a cuckoo's call. No, it was Norman putting on his crash helmet on the day when the hanging baskets went up. These were large, colourful affairs. The village idiot feared that one falling on his head would be the end of him. He was determined to live to be a hundred and that meant never taking a risk. So when outside, he wore his helmet from April until the end of September.

It was the convent that first caught Henrietta's eye. Or rather her ears. It contained a cheerful group of nuns who slept three to a bed to be within easy reach of each other. Their favourite game was ring a ring a roses because they liked holding hands. They also liked glimpsing each others knickers when their skirts billowed. The lawn was kept quite long for comfortable landings.

The grounds were large, with a vegetable garden and an orchard. Sister Martina was the Reverend Mother. She was buxom, with white hair and prominent teeth. She had summoned Sister Adela and was peering gravely at a letter. The lawn had inadvertently become the scene of the young girl performing her special duty. One that demanded a certain creative participation.

"I always said your vocal contribution was too theatrical," said her companion. "And now you've really done it. It's attracted the attention of that newcomer Miss Tobias. She looked into the garden and you can guess what she saw."

Her listener nodded ruefully. "A bouncing bare bottom."

"Exactly."

The young girl was amazed. "How could she? The wall is seven foot high."

"Apparently there was an old chair nearby and she

stood on it. Why people don't take their discarded stuff to the tip I don't know. The point is she has done. And she is making a complaint to the police and Church authorities of obscene exposure. Why on earth didn't you go into the potting shed? I know the mattress is a bit lumpy but it's perfectly adequate."

"Because the man -"

The Reverend Mother threw up her hands. "Don't tell me who he was. I don't want to have to tell lies."

"He met me on the lawn. He demanded to be paid immediately. It was a nice day and the grass was dry. So I thought - ." The speaker turned pale. "What are we going to do?"

"I will tell her we are holding a full investigation. That will buy us some time."

"Well, I don't see how anybody can be identified by their bottom."

Sister Martina scrutinised the letter. "Apparently there is a large pimple on the left cheek."

The young girl screwed up her eyes in thought. "No, it is on the right."

"Well, your right, her left. Don't forget she was facing you."

The Reverend Mother let out a long sigh. It was all Sister Beatrice's fault. Vivid dream indeed! She had claimed God had appeared at the end of her bed. And in ringing tones announced the winning numbers of the next National Lottery draw. They had burned into her brain. On waking, she had quickly written them down. 1, 3, 7,10, 12, 40. Everybody had laughed. Well, as much as you can in a convent. But then they studied the figures and gasped. There was one God. His son rose on the third day. There were seven deadly sins, ten commandments and twelve disciples. And Jesus had been cast into the wilderness for forty days.

Sister Martina bought the ticket and locked it in her

desk. Then she planned the coming celebration. Just falling on your knees to give thanks was not good enough. Not for a windfall like that. No, it was a miracle. So everybody would go to Lourdes to show their gratitude in style. It would remind other pilgrims that God healed finances as well as bodies. She booked berths on the ferry for the entire party. Each with its own porthole. And hired a luxury coach to be waiting at Calais. At the end of the journey would be a four star hotel. A wonderful change from their own little stone cells. It cost an entire month's budget but now they could afford it.

The convent was awash with excitement as the draw approached. Never one to leave anything to chance, the Reverend Mother doubled early evening prayers. It might be hard on the knees, but God needed to be given a nudge. Just in case he had forgotten. They watched the numbers come up transfixed. Sadly their efforts were neither loud enough nor long enough. They failed to even win ten pounds.

The next day Sister Martina was gloomily studying a growing pile of bills. There was a sudden knock on her door. It was Adrian Fox the butcher. He was normally a cheerful young man but now he was sombre. Having been put off twice, he really needed paying but there were no funds. The Reverend Mother was trying to explain her predicament when there came another knock. It was Sister Adela. She wanted the key to the sewing room. She had torn her habit and borrowed sister Charity's. It was a size too small and greatly accentuated her alluring curves. Adrian had a thing about nuns. He always went for kisser-gram girls dressed like them. But this was the first real one who was attractive, he had met. And was she attractive. He appeared to forget about his money. Especially when she bent over the desk to pick up the object of her visit.

Her lifted hem revealed a pair of beautifully shaped ankles. The watching Reverend Mother raised grateful eyes to heaven. God certainly moved in mysterious ways. Ok, he'd made a mistake on the lottery. But now he had sent in her youngest nun to save them. She rose to her feet.

"I have to do my rounds. Sister Adela will entertain you." Passing the puzzled girl, she murmured "The convent is in your hands. It is God's will."

The door had barely closed when she was in Adrian's. She was a dedicated member of her Order. But something had been missing from her life. Within five minutes she was discovering what it was. She would never look at Sister Martina's sofa in the same way again.

Some men would have kept such a valuable secret to themselves. Why share it? Or rather her? But others are never able to keep their mouths shut. And Adrian was one of these. The first one to hear it was James Cannon of the Nag's Head. A skilful listener and extractor of information. And of course, an excellent spreader of gossip. Adrian arrived at opening time having naturally worked up quite a thirst. He and the landlord were alone but he still spoke almost in a whisper. "I've just been paid by the nuns."

"That's nice."

"No, by a nun."

"I'm glad you got your money."

"It was in kind."

"What do you mean in kind?"

"What I say, she paid in kind."

"Who did?"

"This young nun." The speaker put down his glass. "James, have you ever seen a pretty young nun pull her habit over her head?"

"I can't say I have."

"Never mind the Hanging Gardens of Babylon. It's one of the wonders of the world. No, THE wonder of the world."

"You mean she stripped off ?"

"Yes, right in the Reverend Mother's office."

"Was she there?"

"Of course not. She'd left her alone"

"That was very remiss of her."

"No, I think it was intentional."

"So you mean it could happen again?"

"The signs are there."

James dropped his tea towel in mid polish. "Move down the bar," he commanded. Hot conversations had to take place at the far end. Out of hearing of the upstairs room where his wife was glued to the television. Petal rarely missed a programme. But had an uncanny ability to listen to it with one ear while taking in what was being said downstairs with the other. Yet she rarely ever ventured there. Only to get a pickled egg or packet of crisps during the commercials.

Safely out of range, the landlord demanded a blow by blow account. And there were a lot of them. His was a riveted figure as the butcher obliged. He'd heard plenty of stories in his time as those in his profession do. But never one quite like this. At least a true one. He did not doubt for a moment that what the speaker described had taken place. He was still partly in shock and kept pinching himself. James was delighted for his customer. He always shared in their joys and triumphs as well as their sorrows. But this was one he felt he would like to be more involved with. No, he must not think like that. It was obviously a one-off. But was it? He'd heard the convent was in financial trouble. This would certainly be a way out of it. He could tell that Adrian would go back for a second helping. And a third and a fourth. And what about the others in the village?

Upright citizens one and all? He gave an ironic laugh. They'd be queuing round the block.

After the butcher's first visit, meat began arriving free at the convent or at vastly reduced prices. And money on postage was saved as well. Adrian always came to be settled up in person. And then word of his good luck began to get around. One after another, tradesmen and shop keepers found it most refreshing to be paid in kind. And then others came offering to do odd jobs. Even picking up leaves. The convent could have been painted several times over. It had been perfect but now this Henrietta woman had arrived.

Sister Adela finally told the Reverend Mother she needed a rest. She was being worn out by the experience. "I'm feeling exhausted." she said plaintively. "I wish somebody else could be the paymaster for a change"

Her companion eyed her severely. "We've been through this before. You know everybody else here only likes girls."

"It's this having two sets of accounts. Why can't we go back to just having the official one? When we actually pay people in cash? We've got rid of our debt."

"Yes, but now we're making a handsome profit. The Church reimburses us for our so called bills."

"But this complaint could uncover everything. And I am in the middle."

"You are quite safe child. It is just as difficult to identify a pair of legs as it is a bottom. Especially when all that's visible are the soles of the feet. Think of your duty. We have to watch our finances." She gave the young girl an encouraging smile. "But you must try to be quieter. After all, we are decorous by profession."

Sister Aldela's eyes flashed. "It's all very well for you to say that. You're the one who told me to give it extra feeling if anyone was owed over a hundred."

There was happily no religious bigotry in Hatchett. The Reverend Ronnie Perks felt great sympathy for Sister Martina when he heard the news. Even though she had refused to divulge the lottery numbers to prevent the protestants from getting a share. As it turned out, he had saved a pound. He too had received a letter after his last communion at St Andrews which Henrietta had attended. Apart from being irritated by the indisciplined farting of the choir, she had been horrified at a worshiper burping irreverently after gulping her sacrament. This was Ada Smith who blamed Dora Ford for poking her in the back. The pair sat on opposite sides of the front pew and always tried to be first at the alter. Ada had won. But her lack of breath and the stabbing finger, had made the wine go down the wrong way.

The vicar was quite blasphemous for a man of the cloth. He claimed he bore a cross just like his saviour. He had been mentally nailed to it for seven years. It took the form of his wife Hilda. It was an apt expression as her arms were often held wide in supplication. Would he do this? Would he do that? Why hadn't he done this? Why hadn't he done that? To be fair, she had a point. Whenever she wanted action, he was preparing a sermon. These took hours although each only lasted twenty minutes if the congregation was lucky. He insisted that God must be put first. At times, she felt she didn't even come second. Or third.

She'd met him when he was a dashing young curate. Now he had become portly which was exactly the right description. Port had a lot to do with it. Ronnie liked dispensing what he cheerfully called Christ's blood. Particularly to himself. He had goblets of wine scattered around the rectory. And he was generous to his flock. There was nothing like a decent gulp to make the service go with a swing. Several of the more elderly had given up kneeling. They found it difficult to get back on their feet. Hilda felt he held his chalice with twice the tenderness she ever received. Although she conceded he did have his moments. Especially after going up to the colonel's for a whisky and watching one of his handyman's videos. Then he would return with the most unholy look in his eye.

Chapter 2

Arthur and Angela Broad ran the post office and they too quickly fell foul of Henrietta. They supplemented their meagre income by making home videos. These were put up for sale in brown envelopes on the top shelf. Taking a leaf out of the Sainsburys and Tescos book, they advertised them as cheap in-house brands. Broad's Basics they were labelled but in this field, basic can be best. They sold like hot cakes. Gavin the postman filmed them in their upstairs quarters. He was known for his steady hand. He became adept at holding the camera with one while mopping his brow with the other. He was not paid, but always had a shower with Angela afterwards.

There were few props. Angela's impressive breasts provided most of the scenery. In 'Anyone For Afters?' Arthur appeared to be having them for lunch. And in 'Dizzy In The Desert' they doubled as camel humps. The actors were too breathless for much dialogue but Arthur could grunt in several different accents.

The leading lady would thump anybody who mentioned porn. She was an artiste. One who communed with nature. Acting was freer without clothes. The human form was a thing to admire and it certainly was in Hatchett, as their sales indicated. She might be rather top heavy, but if you've got it, flaunt it. That was her watchword.

Innocently browsing, Henrietta had chosen 'Mount Olive.' She adored biblical landscapes. So seeing a naked newsagent's wife on all fours with a pink skinned Arthur scampering along behind, was a great shock. She had to watch it twice to make sure she could believe her eyes. Then she looked at the title more closely. Suddenly it made sense. It was ' Mounting

Olive.' Within minutes, she was delivering her letter threatening to write to the Postmaster General. She received a swift refund and a free Kit-Kat but left seething with indignation.

Regaining the street, she thought hard. Now she knew why God had sent her on a mission to clean up Hatchett. What an amazing place it was. It had such an impressively genteel air. Yet half the time its inhabitants wore less clothes than her tribe in the jungle used to do. Mounting Olive indeed. And that church. More like an off licence. And what about the convent? Nothing more than a bordello. She would stick her nose into every nook and cranny to bring the village back to the Lord.

What she required was an ally and who better than her landlady? Mavis Pitts was as short as Henrietta was tall, but just as thin. Her narrow features rarely broke into a smile. This was understandable. Her husband had fled on the last day of their honeymoon. And as she neither smoked nor drank anything more than a small glass of sherry, she had nothing else in life to cheer her.

She was a cleaner and stuck her nose in everywhere. It was equally as busy as her tenant's. She worked at the pub, the restaurant and the church.

Henrietta was soon spending more time downstairs with Mavis than upstairs on her own. The pair would sit side by side on the sofa. They often shuddered at the thought of their predicament. They were surrounded by every failing of human nature. You name it and somebody in the village was at it. The cleaner agreed firmly with the missionary. There was nothing else for it. They must return Hatchett to God.

They had their first good talk the day Henrietta had been to the convent. She appeared in the doorway so shocked, Mavis had to help her off with her coat. She knew her friend's religious sensibilities.

"You look like you've seen a vision" she said.

The stunned figure took time to answer. "I have. I certainly have."

"What was it?"

"A behind."

Her listener blinked. "A behind?"

"You know, what you sit on." The speaker had a far away look. "It was rising and falling, rising and falling."

"Where?"

"On the convent lawn." The shocked spectator sank into a chair. "It was bare."

"What was? The lawn?"

"No, no the behind."

Mavis had a flashback to her honeymoon. "It can't have been on its own."

"No it wasn't. There was another pair of legs, long legs."

"That's dreadful. And in a house of God too."

"It certainly is."

"What are you going to do?"

"Report it to the police and write to the Reverend Mother. And I'll do it now. While everything is fresh."

Mavis excitedly provided pen and paper and watched her new friend scribble. The cleaner's face puckered. "I wonder whose it was?"

"It doesn't matter. It shouldn't have been there."

"But it does matter. Virtually every man in the village is married. That behind was almost certainly committing adultery."

Henrietta laid down her pen. "Then we must definitely find its owner. He has a large pimple on the left cheek."

"But how? We can hardly call a parade."

"God will show us the way."

The pair ran through the list of suspects. Virtually

16

everybody was in the frame, apart from Norman that is. He had returned from collecting his payment for delivering newspapers with coins jingling in his pocket. Sister Adela had gently put out her hand, but when he saw there was no money in it, he became quite upset. Maybe he was not an idiot after all.

Chapter 3

The landlord of the Nags Head had his own lighting up time. This was when the pub shut. But only after ensuring there was no chink in the curtains. Once these were checked, the puffing began. The Inside Smoking Club held regular meetings. There were around a dozen members. They sat clutching a convivial glass, revelling in the thickening atmosphere. Among them was constable Terence Tompkins. Or PC 42 as he was known. Funnily enough, that was his age and also the number of pints he drank a week. Six a day. He was on his fifth as he chatted to the Reverend Perks. Flowers were going missing from the graveyard. Young Matt Simpson was the suspect. He was courting and could regularly be seen, bouquet in hand, knocking on Betty Dodd's door. Especially after funerals.

"Talking of blooms," said the constable. "If you gave every one in the village to that Tobias woman she wouldn't crack a smile."

"I was thinking more in the shape of a wreath," replied the vicar.

His companion looked up. "That's not very godly."

"Sometimes the Lord needs to smite one of his flock." The speaker's face hardened. "I don't mind her attending my services. The bigger the audience the better, but on Sunday she started tutting. Not just under her breath. Quite loudly."

The policeman frowned. "What was she tutting about?"

"My tankard."

"Your tankard?"

"Yes, I keep it behind the alter in case I get thirsty."

"A sip of water for a parched throat eh?"

"Of course. But she thought it was beer."

His listener's mouth dropped open. "She didn't?"

"She did and actually it was. I don't do it every week," he added hastily. "It was just that on this occasion, the bottle was closer than the tap."

"My goodness, what happened?"

"She accosted me afterwards. I managed to convince her it was a reflection from the stained glass windows. At least I think I did. Luckily the sun was shining through them, but she's been giving me odd looks ever since."

The constable nodded sympathetically. "A close run thing by the sound of it. She's certainly putting herself about."

"She definitely is. And if you're not careful, she'll be taking over your job."

The uniformed figure shifted uncomfortably. "She already has. She says if I don't book those cars parked on double yellow lines by the cross roads she'll write to the Chief Constable. She feels in danger passing them on her bike."

"But we always park there."

"That's what I told her." He frowned deeply. "And there's something else."

"What?"

"She saw somebody having their bill paid at the convent. She heard a noise and looked over the wall."

"Yes, I heard."

The constable took a swig. "Most of us would have said good luck to whoever it was and ducked down. But she has made an official complaint and I'm duty bound to investigate. She could only provide a scant description. She said it would have been better if her chair had been a bit higher."

"We have to be grateful for small mercies."

"Exactly. I can name plenty of suspects without leaving this chair."

19

The vicar sighed. "Maybe even you and me."

The constable eyed him carefully. "Yes, maybe us too." He called to James who was not above suspicion either. "Two whiskies please landlord and you'd better make them large ones."

Cleaning the pub next morning, Mavis sniffed the air. She gave an involuntary shudder. Tobacco. A flagrant breach of Heath and Safety rules. Her nose twitched feverishly. Yes, there had been smoking. Lots of it. She'd believed the windows had been opened to keep her moving. The mornings were fresh but no, it was to hide the tell- tale smell. Well, they hadn't fooled her. There were no longer ten commandments but eleven. Thou shalt not smoke inside a public place. Henrietta must be told.

That afternoon with Mavis by her side, the missionary got to work. 'Dear Mr Cannon. I have been informed'. No, that wouldn't do. 'It has been brought to my notice that cigarettes are being illegally consumed on your premises. This will produce victims of passive smoking as well as damaging the health of the perpetrators. There could well be legal proceedings. In the first instance I am writing to your brewery. It may feel you are no longer fit to hold a licence'.

James stared at the piece of paper in horror. He resembled Captain Billy receiving the black spot in Treasure Island. It was enough to make anybody reach for the rum. Instead he had a steadying whisky. He was growing used to his regulars bemoaning the presence of that Tobias woman. Now he was joining the club. And what a club. The Reverend Mother, Reverend Perks, Arthur and Angela Broad and PC 42. Who was going to be next? The whole village was becoming on edge. But who had shopped him? That was the trouble with small communities. Everybody knew what everybody else was doing. Except of course, who was involved in hanky panky on the convent lawn. Nobody would own up to that. Certainly he wouldn't.

Chapter 4

Breathing fire and brimstone was taking its toll on Henrietta. She began to suffer flushes. Hot ones and cold ones. So she went to see Doctor Roberts. Ironically George looked the sickest person in the village. He was a sparse man with grey hair swept back from a high forehead. He had an almost deathly pallor. Yet he saw this as an asset. It made his patients look healthier.

His wife had narrowly missed marrying a surgeon. The former nurse felt she had come down in the world by ending up with a general practitioner. To her, wielding a knife was far more glamorous than a stethoscope. Even if it created a lot of blood. He became used to her hang dog expression. She only lost it when he gave her one of his home made concoctions. Then he could have been the world's top consultant although he always needed a really long rest afterwards.

He carefully put an ashtray piled with dog ends into a desk drawer. Leaning across it, he swung the open window backwards and forwards to freshen the air. Then in his most authoritative voice called "Come."

The door opened and the missionary entered. Her nose immediately twitched. No, it couldn't be. A doctor smoking in his surgery? She sniffed again and frowned. He waved her to a chair. Next to it on a sideboard, was a bowl of fruit. She admired their quality. The apples and bananas lacked a single blemish.

"They're plastic," he explained. "I put them there to encourage a proper diet. I don't touch the stuff myself. Real ones would just go rotten." He put his hands together. "What can I do for you?"

Although they had not met before, he knew about

Miss Tobias. He'd had the odd snigger over her antics but now she was his patient, he'd better watch out. She explained her problem. He clicked his tongue sympathetically and asked her to roll up her sleeve. Yes her blood pressure was high, very high.

He had a sudden idea. What she needed was a holiday. That was it. A good long holiday. Greece maybe, or Italy. Or somewhere much further afield like Thailand. A thrill ran through him. He would be Hatchett's hero if he pulled this off. Yet he felt a chill in the air. Her voice went cold at his suggestion. "I have had enough of being abroad thank you. I am perfectly happy here."

This was not strictly true of course. Lots of things in the village made her seethe, but God had chosen this path for her and she would see it through. He wrote out a prescription. "Take two of these a day. Come back in a week and we'll check you again." He made a mental note not to have a cigarette until after she'd been. "Surgery starts at eight," he added with great emphasis.

Out in the road, Henrietta decided to drop him from the list of her suspects. He didn't look to have enough energy in him. Her eyes narrowed. But some men had hidden stamina. No, she wouldn't cross him off just yet but he was not among her front runners.

That evening the doctor popped into the Nag's Head for a pint. As he sipped, he told the landlord of the missionary's visit. And how he had urged her in vain to take a holiday.

James wiped a tankard thoughtfully. "Why not send her on one of your other trips? It could be very beneficial for us."

His companion looked doubtful. "I don't know. There could be repercussions."

"But they wouldn't be great. And she could end up in a different frame of mind."

"She wouldn't do it."

"Why should she know? No names, no pack drill. Tell her it's a pick me up. It certainly picked us up didn't it?"

To enliven their lives, the doctor sent favoured patients on what he called technicolor journeys. Not too big a dose for them fly. That was the important thing. Just enough for sprinting along the runway. He pensively rubbed an ear. How would the missionary react to LSD? The experience might well make her more amenable to Hatchett's lifestyle. The odds were long of course. It was difficult to change the mind of a religious fanatic but there was a glimmer of a chance. He came to a decision. He would do it. And on her next visit. James leant across the bar and shook his hand warmly. And for good measure, patted him heartily on the back. The strength of it made George's eyes water.

Miss Tobias was first into the surgery the following week. The doctor greeted her with relief. He was desperate to light up. Yes, her pressure was back to normal. The tablets were working but what about a tonic to follow? An ideal one to stimulate the brain? He handed her a small capsule containing liquid. She took it and put it in her bag without comment. Coloured water no doubt. Patients were always being fooled. George could not believe his luck. He had never expected it to be this easy, but all the same he had to issue a warning. It was the ethics of his profession. "It's best to take it in the evening when you're doing nothing," he said. "And it's really a ground floor medicine. If you take it upstairs, make sure the windows are shut."

But the object of this advice appeared not to be listening. Her nose was twitching. She was again sure somebody had been smoking and it could only be the doctor. If so, it was another flagrant breach of health and safety rules. But caution was the key word. She would get a second opinion. Mavis must make an appointment and have a sniff too.

As Miss Tobias walked home, she shook her head sadly. What a task God had set her. Already the vicar and the Reverend Mother had been found wanting. And the doctor was about to join them. There was no doubt it was tobacco. Three main pillars of society! And what about that bottom? Every time she closed her eyes it bounced cheekily into view. It had begun to torment her. She felt certain she passed it every day. Hatchett was such a small place and its owner was in its midst. She sensed it safely in its trousers laughing at her. She clenched her long bony fingers in frustration.

Mavis agreed to help. If anybody knew a cigarette had been lit, it was her. She also inspected Henrietta's tonic and did not like the look of it. She was no expert on drugs but rumours of LSD trips were rife. Especially after the colonel on the hill had tackled an imaginary German tank in his kitchen. She broached her fears but her friend's mind was on other things. She would put it in her cupboard. It would be safe there. It could prove to be a valuable weapon in the future.

Chapter 5

An Italian called Ant ran the Old Venice restaurant. His real name was Antonio but he had dropped the second half to blend in with the English. Yet he couldn't hide his native hot blood over football. He was a fervent supporter of Roma and the day they beat mighty Milan sent him into ecstasy. He put on a sportsman's dinner for the village to celebrate. His wife was away, so he paid his two waitresses five pounds extra to appear topless. Tracey and Linda were generous girls and only too anxious to please. They needed the money. For another two pounds fifty they agreed that Gavin with his steady hand, could paint their breasts as footballs. These were roundly shaped which provided an impressive result. So much so that they asked for two pounds fifty for each one. An admiring Ant happily forked out.

"If only we had three," said Tracey wistfully pocketing her reward.

Their presence was kept a surprise but guests were given a hint on their invitations. 'Handling a football will evoke an instant red card,' these warned. There were gasps of delight when the girls appeared. They had been endowed more magnificently than anybody else in the village and they knew it. The only one to come close was Margaret Powers but the shape of hers were more fitting for a rugby dinner.

The proceedings became most convivial and as the temperature rose, so did the voices. A merry hum drifted down the street where the missionary and the cleaner were taking a walk. Attracted by the noise, they peered through a partly open curtain. They recoiled in horror, but quickly found themselves drawn back. The ample assets of Tracey and Linda were bobbing above the heads of the diners as they dispersed jugs of wine. It was hardly a Roman orgy but the guardians of Hatchett's morals gasped in unison.

"Wherever you go in the village," declared Henrietta, "There's either a bare breast or a bare bottom."

"And the behind we're looking for will be in there somewhere," replied Mavis with conviction.

Her companion nodded sombrely. "The problem is which one?"

Yet the pair agreed regretfully there was nothing they could do about the party. It was a private one but a letter to the licensing bench would not go amiss. Nor would a quiet word with Ant's wife Rosa when she returned.

Invited to tea, her matronly figure heaved with indignation as her hosts unfolded their story. All three firmly agreed that men had to be kept an eye on. And talking of men, Henrietta and Mavis exchanged glances. Should they? They should. The missionary explained in hushed tones what she had seen at the convent. Did Rosa have any ideas?

Rosa did, but she would need time to think. And the first one in her thoughts as she walked home, was her own Antonio. He took his specially made pizzas to the nuns and he never came back with money. He said they were gifts. They would make him closer to God when he reached heaven. Her brow furrowed. Or was he getting a different kind of heaven here on earth? She was too shrewd to ask him outright. But Mama Mia, he would have to be watched carefully. The party was a different matter. She barely had time to take her coat off before confronting her husband.

"Antonio."

"Yes my dear?"

"There is a shortage of brassieres in the village,

27

yes?"

Her listener looked puzzled. "A shortage of what?"

"Brassieres."

"I don't know."

"There must be. I learn Tracey and Linda did not wear any for your party."

Ant tried to sound off hand. "Oh that."

Rosa put her hands on her hips. "Oh that, oh that, oh that. Is that all you can say? We are a good family. What would our mothers think?"

Her husband uttered a silent prayer of thanks that they were both dead. He opened his hands. "Rosa, it was a little fun for my friends."

"Fun eh? And how much did this fun cost? I know those girls. They would not show their assets for nothing."

"A few pounds."

"How many?"

"Twenty."

"Antonio, we have a business to run. We are wasting our money." She stared at him intently. "So no more free pizzas for the convent."

"But -."

"There are no buts. Do you understand?"

The crestfallen figure could only nod but then he looked on the bright side. That was the one place not to be at the moment.

Chapter 6

Constable Tompkins had no back door to his cottage. So when he saw the missionary coming up the path, he got out of the kitchen window. By the time she was rattling the knocker, he was striding away down a side ally. This happened several times. He was also very careful about answering the phone. He knew what she wanted. To find out how his investigation of the convent was going. So far it was nowhere and that was how he intended it to stay. They played cat and mouse throughout the village but Henrietta was not daft. She was used to dealing with wily African chiefs and she knew PC 42's weak spot.

So steeling herself to enter licensed premises, she walked into the Nag's Head shortly after it opened one morning. She knew he would be having his first pint. He was alone at the bar.

"A lemonade please landlord," she said calmly, taking the stool beside her quarry. He appeared to be having difficulty focusing on his glass. It was too full to be gulped down in one so he could flee. Her voice penetrated his ear.

"Good morning constable."

He found himself agreeing it was. Although in truth, to him it had suddenly become absolutely ghastly. His companion decided there was no point in beating about the bush. "How is your investigation going?"

"Very well."

"Are there any results yet?"

"No."

"Then it can't be going very well." She paused. "Maybe you need more help. I could ask the Chief Constable for reinforcements."

"No, no." the uniformed figure replied hastily. "I

can do very well on my own. I really can."

"It doesn't seem to be so."

"Well actually, I'm going to see the Reverend Mother this afternoon. She has been investigating too. I am sure she will have news for me."

Henrietta looked at him sternly. "I certainly hope so. Whoever it was can't be allowed to get away with such obscene behaviour. It sets such a dreadful example."

Constable Tomkins lived up to the reputation of PC Plod as he made his way to the convent. He put one leaden foot in front of the other. In the past, he had had a spring in his step when visiting but the reason then had been entirely different. Oh yes, entirely different.

Sister Adela let him in with downcast eyes. She led the somewhat bashful visitor along the corridor to the Reverend Mother's office. The buxom figure rose from behind her desk and offered a limp hand. He shook it gingerly as his guide departed. He took the seat offered across from her.

"What a splendid afternoon," she said, looking out of the window at the scurrying clouds.

"Yes, splendid."

"Nice and fresh."

"Yes, nice and fresh."

"Not too cold."

"No, not too cold."

"Quite warm really."

"Yes, quite warm."

Sister Martina stared at her companion intently. "And how is your trail? Is it warm?"

"No, stone cold."

She heaved a sigh of satisfaction. "Good. That's how it should be. That Tobias woman told me she was reporting the incident to the police but I knew how you would handle it. My own investigation achieved a similar result. Now it can all blow over."

Her visitor looked glumly at the floor. "I'm afraid it won't."

The Reverend Mother gave a frown. "What do you mean?"

"She's like a dog with a bone. She won't let go. I've been avoiding her but she nailed me this morning. That's why I'm here" He scratched his nose pensively. "She's threatening to ask the Chief Constable for reinforcements if I don't produce a result."

"But how can you? If neither of us know the identities of those involved?"

"She's not stupid. She knows we're not making an effort. If you'll excuse the expression, she thinks we're sticking two fingers up at her. All we have to do is find the nun which should not be difficult, and then make her talk."

"This is not the Spanish Inquisition. We can't put her on the rack."

"What worries me is if the missionary starts digging around, she'll find more than one person's involved. She's already suspicious. You could end up being accused of running a brothel. And if that gets out, you can bet even the Pope will hear about it."

His listener paled as his words sunk in. There was a long pause. Finally she broke it. "What can we do?"

He put his head in his hands, forcing himself to think hard. Suddenly he leapt to his feet and began pacing excitedly. "I've got it! A vow of silence" He stood before her. "You all take a vow of silence. Then nobody can ask you anything. It's the perfect answer."

The Reverend Mother shook her head sadly. "That was my first thought but we belong to the wrong Order."

"Then change it."

"You can't just change Orders like that."

"Then how about a period of meditation? Say six

months. That would take the sting out of everything."

"No, I'm afraid that wouldn't work either."

His mind continued to race. "What about suggesting she saw a mirage? It was bright and sunny. It could all have been her imagination."

"What? In the middle of April? Don't be so silly .And what about the moaning?"

"The breeze rustling the leaves."

"This is a waste of time. She wouldn't believe it for a minute."

Sister Martina rose and began walking up and down in frustration. "This convent does nothing but good for society. Why didn't this woman have a quiet word with me and leave it at that."

"Don't feel picked on. She's getting stuck into everybody. She's already written to the Postmaster General about Arthur and Angela's home movies. It's just as well Sister Adela turned down their offer of a bit part. And I had a close shave. Luckily my truncheon wasn't a prop in the one she saw." He uttered a heartfelt sigh. "And she's complained about smoking in the pub and illegal parking by the cross roads. She's expecting me to take action."

The Reverend Mother appeared not to hear. "She's got it in for catholics. That's what it is. She's an enemy of Rome."

"No, no," protested her companion. "You've got it wrong there." He gave a laugh. "Ask Reverend Perks. She's accused his congregation of unseemly behaviour and of him setting a bad example. Mind you, he was." He shook his head in disbelief. "He was drinking beer during the service."

Sister Martina stopped pacing. "Really?"

"Yes. But he managed to convince her it was water. He said the sun shone on it through the stained glass windows."

His listener resumed her beat. "That woman is enough to drive anybody to drink."

The level of the brandy bottle hidden in her drawer had plummeted recently. She clenched her fists. "We must do something. Otherwise it will be a disaster for the whole village."

PC 42 looked grave. "I agree, but your problem is the most dangerous and has top priority." He got to his feet. "I will do what I can to placate Miss Tobias. Yet I fear the pressure is growing."

The missionary was waiting at his gate. "We have the culprits?"

"No."

"Just as I thought."

"Maybe there aren't any."

"What do you mean?"

"That you imagined everything."

She looked at him blankly.

"You know, a mirage. It was bright and sunny."

A note of contempt crept into her voice. "Is that really the best you can do? A mirage in April ? I thought even you could have done better than that. It is clear that you and Sister Martina are actively working to block my inquiry. 1 can see further action will be necessary."

"You must not be impatient," replied the constable. "We are looking into a very delicate matter. Every nun has to be interviewed and they are unworldly. Conjuring up a picture of what you described will fill each of them with horror."

"I didn't conjure up anything. I saw it. And it was a sight that will surely bring the wrath of God down on the whole village."

Chapter 7

Henrietta and Mavis compiled their first progress report. They agreed that 'progress' was an optimistic word but some had been made. The whole village might be suspects but at least two were definitely ruled out. The village halfwit and Ant. Norman had collected money and the Italian was too dark skinned. He may well have been at it judging by the kind of party he gave, but not when the missionary peered over the wall. The bottom she saw was definitely whiter than white although that was hardly the expression to use.

She was also prepared to absolve Arthur having winced at the sight of his in 'Mounting Olive.' He had definitely not sported a pimple. That was conclusive evidence to her. Until that is, Mavis pointed out you can pinch pimples. That would leave a red spot. But not for long. Henrietta could see the logic of this and the newsagent was put back on the list. Getting used to doing things together, they sighed in unison. It was like looking for a needle in a haystack.

"What we need," suddenly asserted the cleaner, "is expert advice."

Her companion looked perplexed. "What do you mean?"

"A detective. A private detective." She became animated. "There's a firm in the next town. I saw its advertisement in the paper. 'Anybody traced. No job too complex.'

The missionary sounded hesitant. "I don't know, it's a very delicate subject. I think we should leave it to the police. I can always pressurise the Chief Constable."

"But the more officers involved, the more people will clam up."

The missionary could see her point. Mavis brushed

her doubts aside. "Those kind of detectives are used to hanky panky. They're always snooping on husbands and wives. They wouldn't turn a hair."

Henrietta caught her enthusiasm. They had to succeed and would seek whatever help necessary. "Right," she declared with renewed determination, "we will go tomorrow."

Donald Chambers was a worldly man. Few things surprised him in life. Yet he was intrigued by his visitors. He was small in stature and becoming fat due to sitting for long hours at stakeouts. He was almost bald and had a small moustache. He waved the pair towards two rickety chairs in front of his desk. They sat down. He said nothing but raised his eyebrows.

Henrietta and Mavis wondered how to begin. The missionary took the plunge first. "We would like you to trace a behind. Or rather the owner of it."

The detective said nothing but put his hands together.

"We believe it has committed adultery," added the cleaner helpfully."And it was being obscene in a house of God."

Mr Chambers closed his eyes. Either he was going to sleep or he felt a headache coming on. Henrietta took it for concentration and told the whole story. The detective spoke for the first time.

"How many suspects?"

"The whole village."

"If you know the time and date, you have to find what everybody was doing at that moment."

"It is almost impossible now. It happened two weeks ago."

"You should have come to see me sooner." He opened his eyes. "The other clue would be his clothes. Presumably they were nearby. Trousers round the ankles. That sort of thing."

The missionary looked mortified. "I didn't notice."

Her listener nodded sympathetically. "A common fault. You were transfixed by the moving object."

"It seemed to fill my vision."

"Yes, it would. Any distinguishing marks?"

A large pimple."

"That could be removed."

"Yes, we've realised that."

Mr Chambers let out his breath. "I charge a hundred pounds a day. It would be unfair to take your money. It is not often I refuse a job but I think your case is near enough insoluble. However, if you are able to narrow your list of transgressors to a handful, you may call on me again." He stood up and offered his hand." Good hunting. But if you ask me,the only answer is to put up a ladder at each window at bed time and observe the undressing,"

Chapter 8

Colonel Grant sat across from his wife at breakfast in their big house on the top of the hill. He was a burly man with a shock of black hair.

"That Tobias woman is certainly stirring up the village," he said buttering his toast. "And about time too. It's an absolute den of iniquity. Mind you, those Broad videos are entertaining if a little crude."

"I don't know why you watch them with Jenkins."

"I have to show an interest. He has quite a library." He spooned the marmalade. "No, there's been a definite slacking of the moral code. You get a better view of it from up here. I am all for people having fun but Henrietta is good for the place. Just to remind everybody there are rules in life and to keep them on their toes."

Alison topped up her coffee. "She does sound a bit harsh. I suppose it's the missionary in her."

"As I said, it's just the dose of medicine needed. I mean that convent business is a queer one."

"It's so outrageous it must be a rumour. But you've been there once or twice with your firewood so you will hear these things."

The colonel tried to look vague. "Have I? Oh yes. I think I did pop up there once or twice. Only for a moment of course. But," he went on hastily, "I have to emphasise how much I support the woman. Maybe it's my military background but I very much value discipline. Everybody should be an upright citizen and not only on the parade ground."

There was a knock on the door and Jenkins entered. "I've done the early shopping sir, but things aren't right in the village."

His listener laughed decisively. "I know that."

His odd job man appeared to have difficulty thinking straight. "It was only eight thirty but constable Tomkins gave me a parking ticket."

The colonel lent forward. "What?"

"I parked where I always park. Outside the grocer's."

"On the double yellow lines?"

"Yes, but I've never been booked before."

"No, neither have I."

"I thought it was a joke at first but he was deadly serious. He apologised, but said he had to do it. Otherwise Miss Tobias would report him to his superiors. She'd noticed no tickets were being issued." He drew an envelope from his pocket. "And there's this from the landlord of the Nag's Head."

The colonel took it and slit it open. He stared intently at the letter and let it slip from his fingers. His voice seemed to come from somewhere else. "James has disbanded the smoking club. He says he had no option. The missionary has reported him to the brewery."

Alison put down her cup. "Well, I'll just have to put up with you smoking at home."

Her husband suddenly blazed with anger. "That woman should be put against a wall and shot."

"And I'll pull the trigger," added Jenkins with feeling as he sorrowfully made his departure.

"No, shooting is too good for her," replied the colonel watching him go.

"Wait," cut in the figure at the end of the table. "I'm confused. A moment ago you were giving her your full support. She was the best thing to happen to Hatchett. What was needed was iron discipline. Now you want her dead."

"That ticket was completely unnecessary. There was no need for those lines to be there. We were all agreed on that. Especially constable Tompkins."

"But they are there and according to you, the law has to be obeyed."

"Only when it's sensible. This was a senseless one. Perpetrated by an interfering woman."

"Well you can't say that about the smoking club. You will now all live longer and have healthier lives."

Her husband bristled with indignation. "I am not an uneducated native in Africa. I do not need a missionary to tell me how to live. There is nothing wrong with the odd cigar smoked in congenial company."

"In an illegal place."

"The venue is of no concern."

"Oh yes it is."

"In the eyes of a mistaken government, yes, but not in those of friends meeting quietly together."

"You have to be quiet because you're not supposed to be there."

"Alison, I am not going to argue with you over this dreadful woman. She has come barging into this village telling everyone what to do. I will not tolerate it.And neither will any decent Englishman and there are plenty of us in Hatchett."

His wife looked amused. "What are you going to do? Form a posse and drive her out of town?"

"Look," he said glowering at her. "Don't give me ideas."

Arthur and Angela were studying their own letter. It was from the Post Office. A video sold on the premises had caused a complaint. Anybody was entitled to make home movies but those sold under its banner had to be fit for general viewing. It noted that the one criticised had been removed. The complainant however had provided a list of titles. It would be grateful if a short explanation could be given for each. If these were provided, no further action would be taken.

"Well, that's fair enough," said Arthur.

"Yes, but we're not out of the wood yet," replied his wife eying the top shelf. "It would be a pity if we had to withdraw them all."

"We cannot afford to do that."

"Well then, we'll have to find suitable descriptions."

Her husband took down a handful. Their current best seller was 'Sally's Haystack Surprise.' The newsagent thought hard and scribbled. Rural comedy. Young farm girl sticks pitch fork into sleeping tramp.

Angela looked over his shoulder." Not bad."

He picked up another. 'Henry's Hot Potato.' A quick frown and he wrote: cooking caper. Husband learning how to handle Sunday lunch. His wife whistled in admiration. But what about the third? Tracey's Great Tits? That could be tricky. A bird's nest immediately floated into both their minds. Fledglings flying around a Spring garden. It took an hour to finish the list. The pair were satisfied with the result.

"We'll just have to be more careful in future," warned Arthur. "We can't keep that woman out of the shop, but from now on these will have to go under the counter. And then offered only to select customers."

Angela laughed. "You mean the rest of the village."

"Yes, but we can't take any chances. One slip up with the missionary about and we could lose our livelihood."

Chapter 9

The vicar strode into the Nag's Head. "A pint of best James and put a whisky chaser in it."

"It's a little early for that, isn't it?"

"That Tobias woman wants to join the choir."

"I thought you were always looking for recruits."

"Not one like that. She's already breathing down my neck as it is."

"Well she can't do any harm if she's in your hallowed building."

"Can't she? She'll mark the level of the alter wine in no time. We'll all be on half rations."

"Come now, it won't be as bad as that."

"Won't it? She's an absolute menace to society. She's closed down your smoking club, swept Arthur's videos off the shelves and restricted our parking." He took a hefty gulp. "And she's only been here three weeks."

The landlord carefully polished a beer tap. "I agree. But if she gets involved with the church, she'll be less involved with the rest of us."

His listener sounded indignant. "So you want to push her all on to me?"

"That's what men of God are for. To lift the burden from other people's shoulders."

"Christians are taught to share each other's woes."

"I don't remember reading that anywhere. But you're right, Ronnie. She's a force of nature." He stopped polishing and lent his elbows on the bar. "I've been thinking a lot about this Miss Tobias."

"And?"

"The natives got shot of her in Africa didn't they?" He paused. "So surely we can get her out of Hatchett." His companion put down his glass and waited for him to go on. "How did they do it? Remember her saying how she was thrown onto the ground from her stretcher while being taken to hospital with a fever? Shook the life out of her. Well, sadly not quite. But enough to make her come home to recuperate. She believes her bearers tripped, and it was an accident. But was it? If she was as bossy there, as she is here, they could well have done it on purpose."

The vicar looked interested. "What are you getting at?"

"Just that we should set up one ourselves. Nothing too serious. Maybe a broken leg, a few cracked ribs. Something to slow her down. Keep her out of the way. Encourage her to leave."

"That's easier said than done."

"As I said, I've been thinking about it a lot. The key to it is her bike. She goes everywhere on it."

"Well we can't just push her off."

The landlord gave an exasperated sigh. "I'm more subtle than that. No, we'll make her crash."

His listener became enthusiastic. "You mean string a piece of wire across the road?"

"No, nothing suspicious. She has to be forced to do it herself."

"But that's impossible."

"No it's not. But we'll need the help of constable Tompkins."

"We can't ask him to break the law."

"No, no, he will be upholding it."

"When are you going to ask him?"

"Why not now?"

The subject of their discussion appeared in the doorway for his early pint. James placed it before him. "On the house."

"Thanks." The newcomer took a long pull and wiped his lips. "I needed that."

The vicar took a look at his own glass. "I needed mine too."

"Henrietta Tobias?"

The other two nodded.

"She's got me issuing parking tickets. That's bad enough, but she's continuing to insist I investigate that little matter at the convent. It's becoming a very serious business."

The landlord replenished both drinks. And poured himself one for good measure. "Life would be much simpler if she wasn't here."

The uniformed figure agreed fervently. "It would that."

"So all we have to do is remove her."

His look became misty. "If only we could."

"We can."

PC 42's eyes widened as the speaker added, "With your help."

"Mine?"

"Yes, yours." James explained his plan to his riveted listeners. Every morning the missionary free wheeled down the lane from her cottage. The constable would be round the corner at the bottom barring her path. Standing in the middle, his hand would be up to stop her. She would not have time to brake. On either side was a stony ditch. So whichever way she went round him, she would end up in one. It would be a heavy landing but not fatal. She always wore a helmet.

The main participant of the plan was thinking hard. "Why am I stopping her?"

"I was coming to that. There will be a dangerous object in the road which we will organise. Probably a broken branch. It will happen exactly outside Dick Pewter's place. He will be watching and ring for an ambulance if necessary. He was in the St John's Brigade and loves giving first aid."

The vicar frowned. "Aren't you letting too many people in on the plot?"

"Dick's as safe as houses. He goes up to the convent regularly with windfalls. So he's under suspicion like the rest of us."

Ronnie could not contain an unprofessional surge of excitement. "So when will it happen?"

"There's no point in wasting time," replied the landlord. "Tomorrow if it's all right with Terry."

It was.

Henrietta Tobias was due to start out at ten o'clock. The pub was open for coffee. The landlord and the reverend sat nursing theirs by the window. If an ambulance was needed, it would pass outside. Just over the hour later they heard a siren. Then saw the flashing lights. The vehicle careered by on its mercy mission. Ten minutes later came the return journey. Neither of the watchers said a word. They had expected to whoop with delight at the plan's success. Had they overdone it? No, they reassured themselves. Of course not. Whatever the missionary got, she deserved.

They eyed the door expectantly. Dick Pewter was to report as soon as the coast was clear. A stoical figure, he entered with measured tread. Always a picture of studied calm.

"How is she?" the pair chorused anxiously.

"Very shocked, a little bruised, but able to cycle home."

His listeners stared at each other. The vicar broke the silence. "Then who was in the ambulance?"

"Constable Tompkins. He's badly bruised all down his back. It's ironic. He's investigating a bottom but can't sit on his own."

The landlord gaped. "What happened?"

"It started perfectly. We had the obstacle in the road and he was waiting on the spot. Miss Tobias came round the corner bang on time and rode straight into him. She told me afterwards she couldn't make up her mind whether to go left or right. Then it was too late."

The reverend put his head in his hands. "Women drivers."

"Maybe we could get her for assaulting a policeman," said the landlord hopefully.

"No chance" replied Dick. "She'd never deliberately run down the man leading her investigation. And he was in the middle of the road on a bend."

"It was just a thought."

"We've had enough of those at the moment," said Ronnie unkindly. "I suppose," he added, "we ought to go and see Terry."

"I'd leave it for the moment," advised their messenger. "He was saying not very nice things about you both. I told the crew he was delirious."

Constable Tompkins refused to greet visitors lying face down. So his fellow plotters had to wait for three days for him to regain his normal posture. They brought a large bunch of tulips. These had pride of place because there were no other flowers. The patient explained his previous visitor had arrived with daffodils. But then taken them away again. This was Henrietta Tobias. She had come full of apologises but had smelt a rat. The large branch in the road with no tree nearby had not helped. If there was a next time, there must be more attention to detail. She had left in a huff ,and believed the whole village was scheming against her. The operation had been an abject failure.

And worse was to come. PC 42 explained he was going on two weeks sick leave. And being replaced by constable Conrad Marrow. PC 69 preferred six black coffees a day to pints. To keep him alert for duty. And he was just as conscientious off it. A perfect twenty four hour policeman. He too had been to see the patient to organise the take over. His first question was what misdeeds were being investigated? And Pc 42 had found himself revealing everything. He was dreadfully sorry he told his visitors. But the morphine pumped into him had acted like a truth drug. He had been light headed. And at times the concerned figure beside him had appeared to be an angel.

Sadly in real life he was anything but. He was more a terrier sinking his teeth into every crime. And never letting go until it was solved. He had said his first port of call would be Henrietta Tobias. To find out exactly what she had seen. And when. And then to ask every male in Hatchett where they were at that moment. And every answer would be checked and double checked. And those that could not remember, would have their memories jogged. Again and again.

The reverend and the landlord were a chastened pair as they left the hospital.

"It's amazing," said the publican, hands thrust deep into his pockets, "how lives can suddenly get wrecked. A month ago we were all living in harmony and minding our own business. Then whoosh, that woman comes along."

"Yes," mused the vicar. "I've never known anybody so keen to mind other people's business."

James nodded. "And with such drastic results. When you think about it, she's putting several livelihoods at risk and goodness knows what's going to happen at the convent."

"I know. Poor Sister Martina. I met her when the post office opened yesterday and smelt her breath. She had been drinking."

"She's always liked a drop."

"But not that early."

"Well she's in good company. We're all feeling the pressure now."

Chapter 10

Conrad Marrow smoothed down his uniform and knocked on the door. It was opened by Mavis who led him through to the lounge where Henrietta was waiting. He was the same height as the missionary, with bony features and slicked black hair parted in the middle. He waited for the cleaner to leave, but she sat firmly on the sofa beside her friend.

"Don't worry, she's my best witness," Henrietta explained to her visitor who took a chair opposite. His face lit up at the news.

"She is witnessing many things in the village," the speaker went on, "that shows how right we were to start our crusade."

His look faded. "But not at the convent?"

"Oh no. Even standing on my bike she would be too short to look over the wall." She shuddered. "I'm glad for her sake. The sight was horrible."

PC 69 studied his notes. "Constable Tompkins has passed me your statement. Can you add anything at all to it?"

"No. I've racked my brains time and again."

"You say the incident happened around three o'clock. We really need to be more precise. It is the vital factor when we come to establish where everybody was at the time."

"What do you mean?"

The visitor scratched an ear with the tip of his pen. It was a most delicate subject. He had been taught as a cadet how to put a question. But there were questions and questions. How to begin? Finally he took the plunge as tactfully as he could. "The object you saw ascending and descending. How long was it in motion?"

"I don't know. I only got a peep."

"It's important. We have to establish where each suspect was at that exact time. Seconds count." He leaned forward. "Did it give any indication?"

"Did what give any indication?"

"What you were watching. Was it possibly starting or finishing? Or in the middle?"

"This is most distressing. I told you I don't know. I only got a peep."

"Then are you certain of what you saw?"

"Of course I am. When I say a peep, it was quite a long one. Long enough to know precisely what was taking place."

"But we're not being precise are we? That's the problem. The proceedings might say, have started at a quarter two and finished at a quarter past. Or they may just have been going on for a couple of minutes. There are endless permutations. Some suspects could have what appear to be water tight alibis and still have been the offender." He looked earnestly at the missionary. "Think hard. Was there any hint to indicate what stage the proceedings had reached?"

Henrietta's voice had suddenly gone cold. "Not that I could tell."

Constable Marrow's voice became grave. "We have to solve this question if we want to succeed." He tapped his pen on his teeth. "But there are other things we can try." He had just been on a criminal profile course. He turned to Mavis. "You know the men in the village pretty well. Who do you think the most likely candidates are? Does one in particular stand out?"

She answered with conviction. "They all stand out. They're like all men. They're at it all the time."

"I don't think we are," replied the constable a little stuffily.

The cleaner snorted. "You don't know Hatchett. The

48

rumour is the convent pays everybody in kind. And I don't know one male in the village who hasn't been up there at sometime."

"You make it sound as if they are clamouring at the gates."

"They do it very discreetly."

"It doesn't seem like it to me."

"I don't expect they thought anybody would look over the wall."

"The simplest way," said Miss Tobias who was becoming impatient, "is to confront Sister Martina and order her to produce her culprit."

"Constable Tompkins has already tried that."

"He's just as bad as the rest," cut in Mavis. "We don't feel he's made an effort."

The policeman stiffened. "I can't believe that of a fellow officer."

"He's one of the village and they all stick together."

"You're an outsider," emphasised the missionary. "We're relying on you to make the breakthrough."

Chapter 11

PC 42's deputy stood outside the convent. It's tall white exterior was a picture of innocence. He wondered for a moment if the whole thing was a flight of Henrietta's fancy. She had been the only witness. But the ripples her accusations had caused told a different story. He steeled himself and rang the bell. Having been expected, he was quickly whisked along the corridor into the Reverend Mother's presence.

She rose to greet him, hands outstretched, with a kindly smile. It was so good of him to come. But she feared she had nothing to add to what she had told constable Tompkins. By the way. How was he? Was he recovering well?

He was, thank you, replied PC 69 who was determined not to be pushed off course. How was the investigation going into identifying the nun? he asked in return. Sister Martina clasped her hands in front of her in frustration. Slowly, very slowly. It was a difficult subject to broach. They all admitted to frequently using the lawn in fine weather. Apart from their games of ring a ring a roses, they liked to do their exercises there. And some without their clothes so the breeze could blow refreshingly on their nether regions. She looked her visitor steadily in the eye. Could it have been a female rear end? Press ups were particularly popular among the younger ones. She herself, had led a sheltered life and did not know whether they could be told apart from male ones. Putting it as delicately as he could, her visitor said the witness was adamant they consisted of one of each. And suddenly finding hidden courage, added that it was rumoured to be a regular occurrence.

The Reverend Mother's hand was steady as she

poured Earl Grey from the pot into two elegant china cups. "Are you a catholic constable?"

"No. I'm ashamed to say I know absolutely nothing about religion."

"The Holy Spirit is very strong in our Church." She paused for a moment. "Yet I also like another kind, more down to earth. One with some body." She pulled the cork from her brandy bottle and added a generous amount to each receptacle.

Her guest put out a protesting hand. "No, no, I cannot drink alcohol on duty."

She looked at him severely. "Come now. I've given this liquid my personal blessing."

Constable Marrow wavered. "Well I suppose I'm not driving."

"Exactly," replied his hostess, taking an appreciative sip. "It helps lift my own spirit in times of stress."

Her visitor followed suit and smacked his lips. "It does mine too."

The atmosphere gradually became relaxed. They both agreed it was a mystifying case. But for the sake of the convent's reputation and that of Hatchett's, it had to be solved. The constable willingly had another cup. After all, Sister Martina was becoming more co-operative. So much so, that she suggested he might like to interview the nuns himself. He eagerly agreed. But she admitted to being worried they might find his uniform intimidating. She advised him to take off his jacket and tie. And even to kick off his shoes if it made him feel more comfortable. There was no need to go anywhere. She would bring the interviewees to him. They could sit by his side on the sofa. They were much more likely to reveal things in intimate surroundings.

"We will start with the youngest," she said, pouring him a third cup. "She is a shy girl so take your time. You will not be interrupted."

It was quite hot in the office. PC 69 ran a finger round inside his collar and undid a second button. He was glad he had discarded his jacket although he felt less like a policeman. Maybe Sister Martina was right. It could pay dividends.

After a few moments, the door opened and a flustered figure entered. It was Sister Adela. She apologised for keeping the officer waiting. She had been in the shower when summoned. She had flung on the nearest habit which was unfortunately a size too small. And she had not had time to do her hair. Beautifully black and glossy, it tumbled down around her shoulders. She sat herself demurely next to him. When she lent forward to hear his questions, their knees touched. Her large brown eyes were unwaveringly fixed on his. He felt hotter than ever. She seemed to understand and helpfully undid a third button. He was explaining his mission and she nodded sympathetically. It was very difficult. The nuns were so unworldly. They found it hard to imagine what Miss Tobias had seen. She took a deep breath. Perhaps the constable could show her? Silence descended. PC 69 appeared to have difficulty taking this in.

His companion played mother and poured a fourth cup. Adding a liberal amount from the bottle Sister Martina had thoughtfully left beside them. Her interrogator noticed his hand trembling as he picked it up. But each time the contents were becoming easier to drink. The figure beside him gently repeated her suggestion. He discovered his voice had dropped almost to a whisper. She pressed herself against him to hear his reply. He was becoming incoherent. He caught a whiff of perfume. No, it couldn't be. Nuns didn't wear alluring fragrances. It must be incense from the chapel. But it was certainly inviting. He noticed her habit riding up around her thighs. So it was true. She hadn't had time to dress properly. Her voice caressed his ear.

"Show me how it happens. Then all will become clear."

He felt light headed. He sensed his belt was missing. Then he appeared to be parted from his trousers. Everything was in slow motion. He found himself breathing heavily. The only other sound was the creaking of the sofa.

Sister Beatrice had started the whole thing with her lottery numbers. Now she was about to pay her debt. Apart from having vivid dreams, she liked photography. Propping the short ladder under the windowsill, she clambered up. The sun shone over her shoulder into the room. Conditions could not have been better. It was in all respects, a moving scene.

Coming to his senses sometime later, constable Marrow scrambled for his clothes. Sister Adela had already adjusted her habit and gave him a fond smile. He had been very instructive. Now she knew exactly what had happened on the lawn. She took her leave as the Reverend Mother entered. The newcomer held a photograph in her hand. She passed it to him without a word. He stared at it numbly. As he did so, his superintendent's advice flashed into his brain. 'Always be properly dressed when on duty.' He forced back a sigh. He had not seen himself before at that angle. But he could be recognised all right. His uniform beside him had been carefully included.

"Your investigation is finished," said the figure before him in a decisive tone. "And with a most negative result."

Even in his dazed state, PC 69 realised what she meant. Whatever he did with the picture, the convent could produce another. There was really nothing else to say. He felt angry. But at himself. That Reverend Mother was a cool customer. She and the missionary were well matched. And he remembered with a stab of guilt, Miss Tobias would be waiting for him. He had promised to call in on the way back to report his progress. Progress! Well he had certainly made some. But entirely in the wrong direction. And he had a photograph to prove it. Not that he would show anybody. And he was sure Sister Martina would keep quiet too. It was just a matter of assuring the two vigilantes as he called them, that constable Tompkins had been right. There was no way the culprit at the convent could be identified.

The exhilarating effect of the alcohol had worn off. He felt a headache coming as he set out for the cleaner's cottage. And a bigger one was beckoning on the horizon. The missionary would not take his news lightly. It was not a pretty thought. He did not relish being closely questioned. He thought of ducking past, but she was watching from the window and the door was open. Henrietta and Mavis met him in the hall, two pairs of darting, inquisitive eyes.

He laid his helmet on the little side table and squared his shoulders.

"Well?" said the missionary following his every move. "How did it go?"

How did it go? he thought to himself. It didn't go. It had stopped dead. He walked through to the lounge. "I'm afraid I had no better luck than constable Tompkins. Nobody is owning up to anything. In fact the Reverend Mother went as far as to suggest the bottom you saw may have been of the female variety. Apparently the nuns do their physical exercises on the lawn. Sometimes with nothing on."

Henrietta looked as if she was about to explode. "What nonsense. I know exactly what I saw. And I know exactly its gender."

"And it's not going to defy us," added Mavis,

54

showing her support.

PC 69 sank into a chair and closed his eyes.

"You look exhausted," said Mavis. "Would you like a cup of tea?"

The crumpled figure nodded. A drop of brandy in it would have been nice. But he knew there was no chance of getting that here. Miss Tobias bent over him suspiciously and sniffed, making him grateful for the peppermints Sister Martinahad provided for his breath. A frown crossed her face and she sniffed again. "You don't wear perfume do you?"

"No of course not."

"Well you've definitely got some on you."

The officer sniffed at his clothes. "I don't think I have."

"Yes you do, sniff harder."

He did as he was told. A vision of soft white flesh and stresses of long black hair swam into view. He quickly recovered himself. "There is a faint something there. But I've no idea where it came from. It certainly wasn't from the Reverend Mother."

His companion agreed. "No. I can't see her putting on fragrances." Her brow clouded. "Did you interview anybody else?"

"A young nun," he replied without stopping to think. He immediately regretted his rash remark. Miss Tobias had suddenly become alert. She was looking at him in a new light. He had put his clothes back on in a hurry and his uniform showed it.

A cold voice reached his ears. "Where did this interview take place?"

"In Sister Marina's office."

"Was she there?"

"No. She thought I would get on better with the nuns alone."

The missionary was thinking hard. "It would appear

55

so."

Constable Marrow was angry with himself for allowing her to intimidate him. She was just like his mother who would badger away until she got the truth. Well, he couldn't afford to let that happen. He stood up. "I have to go now. I must write my report."

He turned to the doorway to see the cleaner framed in it. "You can't go yet," she said. "I've just made your tea."

He found himself sitting down again. He put in two sugar lumps and stirred. He felt Henrietta's eyes on him. It was hot in the lounge. Almost as hot as in the office. She pulled her chair closer to his. "What did she say? She must have said something."

The constable put a hand to his head. "Say? It's not what she said. It's what she did."

His voice did not seem to belong to him. Without knowing why, he told her exactly what had happened. Maybe he wanted to get it off his chest. That's what catholics did, didn't they? Or so he'd been told. There were two sharp intakes of breath when he had finished. Henrietta's eyes gleamed. She could not contain her excitement.

"So that's it!" she exclaimed. "A brothel! No doubt constable Tompkins was given the same treatment." She looked at Mavis, her bosom heaving. "Half the village will be clients."

"More than half," replied the cleaner, striving for accuracy.

PC 69 sat staring at the carpet. What had he done? Yet it was the right thing for him as a policeman to come clean. It had to come out. But what about his own future? Constable Tompkins was almost fit again so it would mean a return to headquarters. That would stop him getting further into this mess. But he would have to file a report. That was going to be the problem. Yet what he had said, and what he could write, would be two entirely different things. After all, the convent would certainly not spill the beans.

Miss Tobias was sympathetic. She was grateful for what she'd got. She would add the incident to the expose' she was preparing for the Church hierarchy. But he would not be identified. He was only one of what was guaranteed to be a long list. The most important question was, who was the young nun? She had not revealed her name which was what the missionary had expected. Sister Martina was too canny to make such a mistake. But it was then that constable Marrow came up trumps. He had noticed the name sewn inside the habit which had been so wilfully discarded. It had stuck in his brain. It was Sister Bridget.

Miss Tobias leapt to her feet at the news. It was the big breakthrough. She called for pen and paper as PC 69 made a chastened exit. She always did everything by the book. The Reverend Mother was to be duly informed of what had come to light. And that the information would be passed to the relevant authority. Mavis watched over her shoulder as she wrote with furious concentration before signing with a flourish. "There," she said sticking it in an envelope. "At last God's will is being done." She did not for one moment consider that Sister Adela was not wearing her own gown. And why should she?

Chapter 12

Constable Marrow had lodged with PC 42 while on duty in the village. His host had returned the next day to find him packing. "I don't mind telling you I'm glad my stint is over," he said. "Hatchett has such a peaceful air. But it's extraordinary what goes on underneath."

His companion put down his own suitcase. "So how did it go at the convent?"

"You can see my report. It's very brief. I did no better than you."

"I'm glad to hear it. I'm all for a quiet life."

"If only that Miss Tobias was."

"So you had the same trouble with her as everybody else?"

"Yes."

"She wouldn't have been pleased at your lack of progress with Sister Martina. She certainly wasn't with me."

"No, she wasn't," came the hesitant reply.

Constable Tompkins noticed a change of tone. His eyes narrowed. "I expect you were made very welcome at the convent."

"Yes, I was."

"Really good hospitality."

"Yes, excellent."

"They certainly make you very, very welcome."

"They do. They definitely do."

"The thing is not to advertise it."

His listener suddenly looked downcast. "I already have."

"What?"

"I told Miss Tobias I was seduced."

"You what?"

"I told Miss Tobias I was seduced."

PC 42 felt a surge of panic. "Does she know the nun's name?"

He nodded dumbly. "Yes."

"Is all this in your report?"

"Of course not. Do you think I want to commit suicide? It's very mundane and comes to the same conclusion as yours. She promises not to identify me to anyone."

His listener heaved a sigh of relief. "Good. We may yet keep the lid on this. She's doing her own report for the Church. She seems to have given up on us. The best thing you can do is to return to normal duty and say nothing."

"That is my intention exactly."

"I will have to get hold of Sister Martina and certain other people. We will have to act quickly before she can do further damage."

"From what I heard, you didn't do very well last time."

"You don't have to tell me. I've still got the bruises to show for it." His face became grim. "But as the saying goes. If at first you don't succeed, try and try again."

Chapter 13

The vicar had to admit Henrietta was an asset to the choir. They no longer shuffled along to their pews. Instead, with her at their head, they marched crisply. She was always the first to stand for the hymns and kneel for the prayers. And the fervour of her singing put even the baritones to shame. The problem was her eyes. They always seemed to be on him. He expected them to be riveted to her prayer book. But she knew the service backwards and every line of every psalm. Her disapproving gaze was at its fiercest when he dished out the sacrament. It made his already shaky hand, shake a little more. He couldn't understand why. Surely the more of Christ's blood the congregation drank the better?

And then there was his tankard. She kept peering into it. Needless to say since she'd joined, it had only contained water. But it gave the impression she didn't trust him. He, God's specially ordained representative. And again, there was no need to hover while he counted the Sunday morning takings. He'd always paid back the odd fiver he'd borrowed. Apart from the time that odds on favourite had slipped up at Newbury. What annoyed him most, was her giving the impression she was closer to God than he was. When he put the hymn numbers up on the board, she began humming their tunes. She declared it was her personal tribute before the communal effort. Although there was no chance of her voice ever being drowned out. He worried in turn that her presence was making him less of a Christian. When she had to walk home in heavy rain, he hid her umbrella in the hope she would develop flu. A few days in bed would give him a respite. He didn't want it to be too serious. Just a temperature of a hundred and four. He shut his eyes to picture the scene. A pale, clammy face fringed with strands of bedraggled hair protruding from the duvet. A bedside table stocked with bottles of Lucozade among the get well cards. Well, one card. His own. He could not think of anybody else sending one. And what would his say? He knew instinctively. 'Rising too soon will endanger your health. Lie back and think of the Lord. Rest is his most treasured gift for disciples whose strength falters. Take it easy is the motto for recovery.' He didn't want any of that take up thy bed and walk, nonsense.

He sighed heavily. So far it was just a pipe dream. She seemed indestructible. He had watched her leave in the downpour. The rain drops just bounced off her. And talking of bouncing, how far had she got with her investigation? It may have been a coincidence, but several of his male worshippers had begun to pray more fervently. Much more fervently. A wave of sympathy had engulfed him as he watched them go down on their knees. And what about Sister Martina? She had her own brand of Christ's blood. And from what he'd heard, she was really knocking it back. And who could blame her? Every time she shut her eyes she must be seeing the Pope. And he would be wagging a very stern finger at her. The vicar could not help himself trembling slightly. What was going to happen to them all?

Chapter 14

The Reverend Mother looked at the two letters on her desk. One was from the missionary saying she would be contacting the church authorities. The other was from these saying she had been as good as her word. It warned Miss Tobias had been granted an interview with the Mother Superior on her return from holiday at the end of the month. The agitated figure studied the date. That was in exactly twenty one days. She picked up the phone. It was time for action. There were a considerable number of males in Hatchett who had a vested interest in keeping Miss Tobias quiet. The seventh commandment had been taking quite a battering.

It was decided to hold the meeting at the colonel's house at the top of the hill. From it you could see the convent in the distance which was filling the thoughts of all those present. The first to arrive was Sister Martina herself. She had come in person to impress upon everybody the urgency of the situation. After her came the vicar, constable Tompkins, Arthur and Angela Broad, the doctor, James the landlord and Ant. They assembled a little breathlessly. And not just from the exertions of their climb. They sat round the large oak table in the dining room. It was reassuringly solid, unlike their predicament.

The colonel as self appointed chairman, addressed them. And as befitting a military mind, went straight to the point.

"Henrietta Tobias is trying to destroy us all. Our livelihoods are at risk. And in some cases, so are our marriages."

At this, several pairs of anxious eyes were raised to the ceiling.

"We cannot stand idly by and let it happen," he went on. "If anybody doubts the seriousness of what is taking place, they won't after the Reverend Mother spells out the latest developments."

He sat down and Sister Marina stood up. Like him, she laid it on the line. The missionary was now aware the convent paid in kind. And what was worse, the identity of the paymaster. Sister Adela, as they all knew, had some wonderful attributes. But these were her greatest weaknesses. Her generosity and eagerness to please, would make her putty in the hands of investigators. She paused amid an expectant hush. "Miss Tobias is due to tell all to the church authorities in exactly eighteen days. She must not make that meeting."

The speaker sat down and leaning on her elbows, looked each of her companions squarely in the face. They knew they were being challenged to find a solution. But what? Their last attempt to even slow her down had been an abject failure. Constable Tompkins for one, winced at the memory. He would of course, support any plan. But he did not want to be in the front line this time. Everybody began again to look towards their host. He was a man of action. A decisive figure who had planned and carried out military operations. His previous declaration was sadly not viable. Henrietta could not just be put up against a wall and shot. Yet there were plenty of murderous thoughts swirling round the group of worried minds. Staging an accident that would incapacitate, but not actually kill, was again given serious consideration. But the spectre of the earlier failure dampened enthusiasm.

Finally Ant spoke. "What we need is a professional." He felt every gaze swing in his direction. "Our last attempt was very amateurish. We require somebody who knows exactly what they're doing."

Arthur lent forward. "You mean a hit man?"

The restaurateur threw up his hands. "Words, words, words."

The colonel was all attention. "What do you have in mind?"

"I have a cousin in Naples. He is good, how you say in English, at solving problems."

"A Mafia solution," butted in the newsagent. "Rub her out. It's no good scaring her enough just to wet her knickers."

Ant gave the speaker a pained look. "He has ways of helping people change their minds. Or how you say again, leave town."

"How much will he cost?" asked the reverend, picturing having to hand over his Sunday service takings.

Ant shrugged his shoulders. "He will have a free holiday with me. So not much, just the airfare. And that will be split between all of us."

"Well, he can collect our share when he arrives." said Sister Martina.

"No. I'm sorry," replied the restaurateur firmly. "To be fair to everybody, It has to be cash this time."

"If he's staying with you, don't let Tracey and Linda distract him," said the landlord whose memory of the sporting dinner was still vivid.

"Bambini is singled minded," declared Ant. "Nothing will stand in his way. Afterwards, yes, he will celebrate. But before he is as cold as ice."

Angela shivered. "Do we really want her killed?"

"Of course not," replied the vicar speaking for nearly everybody. "But we certainly want her frightened off."

"There is a fine line between the two," said the colonel knowingly. "We will have to give him very strict instructions."

"And make sure he keeps them," added James.

"We haven't asked him yet," the astute Reverend Mother reminded everybody.

"Oh he'll come," replied his cousin with conviction. "He loves England and I know he is available."

"What will he do?" asked Angela.

"He has his methods," Ant replied darkly. "It is not for us to interfere."

"Yes, it is the best way," agreed PC 42. "Let him get on with it."

"But as I stressed," said the military figure, "we have to give him exact guidelines. She has to be put off just enough. We don't want to find her floating face down in the village pond."

Several of his listeners closed their eyes to picture this heart-warming vision.

Sister Martina tapped her fingers impatiently on the table. "We have to get him here first and we're running out of time."

"You're absolutely right," admitted the colonel. "He can't just get off the plane and do the business. He'll have to identify the target and the lie of the land. And then work out his plan of action." He swung round on Ant. "Can he speak English?"

The restaurateur nodded. "A little. But he is a man of few words. He prefers to make others talk. And then listen."

The vicar could see the point of this. "Very wise." He had heard more than enough from the latest recruit to his choir. But this time she would be singing from a different hymn sheet. He sighed happily. Very different indeed.

The colonel broke into his thoughts. "So we're all agreed."

There was a chorus of assent. He looked slowly round the sea of faces. "Remember we are all in this together."

"All for one, and one for all," chipped in Arthur.

There were one or two nervous laughs as the enormity of what they were doing began to sink in.

"Once Bambini is on the plane there is no turning back," warned Ant. "He does not abort a mission."

Time for a drink," announced the colonel who could see one or two nerves needed stiffening. He poured each a good sized whisky and took a gulp of his own. He noticed the Reverend Mother downed hers almost in one. She has the most to lose, he thought as he replenished her glass. But we are not far behind her.

Chapter 15

Bambini sat on the balcony of his smart third floor flat in an affluent suburb of Naples. The sun was sinking and its last rays reflected on his glass of Chianti. The ice tinkled merrily as he took a sip. It matched his mood. He had been languishing too long. Now Antonio had called for help, his adrenalin was beginning to flow. Tomorrow he would be on the plane. But first he had to visit Angelo the printer. He needed a batch of his warning cards put into English. Three lay on the table beside him. His two favourites were 'Leave Tonight Or Die Of Fright' and 'Go Away Or Perish Today' He also liked 'The Knife Is Ready The Hand Is Steady'. A fourth, 'A Tombstone Awaits' could not be used until he had thought of a second line.

He was a stocky figure with a square face and bristly jaw. He put down his drink and did twenty press ups. There was no panting or even heavy breathing. Yes, he was still fit and supple despite his long layoff. Don Carlo had not required his services recently. The city was quiet. So a foreign assignment was most welcome.

He laughed grimly when he remembered what he put on visa applications for reason of visit. 'A little shooting.' Now he could no longer take his weapon because of airport security. But he had an inventive mind. There was more than one way to kill a cat. And if what Antonio was saying was true, this would be a fiery one. He frowned for a moment. He did not like restrictions. They could make a job tricky. The problem was the English were too squeamish. A nice, clean result was what they demanded. Not a drop of blood in sight. He touched his toes several times. The muscles rippling down his back. He had suggested staging a 'suicide.' The woman hanging from a tree in the woods. She could not bare to be ostracised by the village. But his cousin had said no, definitely not. He sighed. He had several other schemes. He would just have to play it by ear. He put his little finger in the left one and wiggled it. Just the place for a bullet. He picked up a foot long piece of cord and handled it lovingly. He could not take a gun, but there was nothing to stop him from carrying this. He fondly recalled all the gurgling noises it had caused. First there was a little struggling. Then the victims turned into sacks of potatoes. You let them down gently. Their faces were all shades of purple. He looked at his own in the mirror. It had cold, smiling eyes. Exactly as a killer should have.

Carefully he packed a small suitcase. He always included a black tie. He liked to officially see off those he had dispatched. It was true to say he had almost attended more funerals than had hot dinners. He wondered what the services were like in England. Knowing its character, there would be plenty of stiff upper lips and dry eyes. He liked to see lots of handkerchiefs being dabbed and hear loud heartfelt sobbing. It was a tribute the deceased deserved. He hoped there would be profound wailing when he went. But there would be many in the queue before him. And was this Henrietta woman at its head? That was the big question. You could only obey instructions for so long if you weren't getting anywhere. He rubbed his thick neck thoughtfully. And the problem was he did not have long. Just a few days.

He tried on his thin leather gloves. They always went with the cord. They clung to his stubby fingers. Absolutely a perfect fit. No matter how many times they had been washed. And they had needed plenty of washing. His preparations complete, he studied the piece of paper before him. It contained every detail of his target provided by Antonio and his fellow conspirators. He had jotted them down one by one as they were relayed over the phone. The first thing he noticed was his victim was a foot taller than he was. He would require a box to stand on if he had to strangle her. Most assassins would have said 'intended' victim. But Bambini had never failed. He was extremely confident that it would remain an unnecessary word.

There would be plenty of opportunity to get her alone as she cycled round the village. He had been told about the previous attempt and tried not to snigger. What a circus! There would be no standing in the middle of the road for him. So typical of a policeman. They were the same in Italy. You could run rings round them. Only Henrietta hadn't. She had gone straight into hers. His eyes narrowed. Had she done it on purpose" Was she cleverer than they thought? He had never underestimated an adversary. That was his strength. He looked grave. This woman would be treated with respect. But it must not be overdone. To start with, as ever, it would be kept simple. The first thing to do was fix her brakes. And the second, to find an obstacle worth running into.

The plane flew into Heathrow on time. Ant and the reverend who was accompanying him, waited patiently in the arrivals lounge. Ronnie felt nervous and had left his dog collar behind. He had never been on the same side as a killer before. The throng of incoming passengers thinned and suddenly a squat figure in a blue suit and dark glasses appeared. Ant threw up his hands. "Bambini!" The cousins hugged each other tightly and capered around. Dancing on the missionary's grave, thought the onlooker sombrely. What have we let ourselves in for? He listened to a torrent of Italian. He feared Ant was getting carried away and was giving him carte blanche. The restaurateur seeing his worried look, clapped him on the shoulder. "I was just asking about all our relatives," he said. "Later we will get down to business."

There was no talk of Henrietta's impending doom on the drive home. They spoke of everything else as the countryside flashed by. Ant gripped the wheel and put his foot down. He gave the impression every second counted. And in truth, these were quickly ticking away.

The restaurant's closed sign was firmly in the window. It was barely dusk but the curtains were already drawn. Behind them waited the reception committee. Ant introduced his fellow conspirators one by one. This was to be their only meeting. No hailing their saviour in the street. He must be as inconspicuous as possible. Not an easy thing to achieve in a small village. He had a variety of disguises and would work mainly after dark. There would be regular progress reports at the same venue. This was chosen because it would be more discreet. Better than everybody trailing up the hill to the colonel's house.

The first of these was set for tomorrow night. When it was hoped, the venture would already be over. Bambini liked to strike quickly. He was already fondling the wire cutters. They would work on the missionary's break cables as soon as it was dark.

The plan was simple. Leaving at her appointed time in the morning, she would free wheel down hill to discover she had no control at the bend. Approaching the cross roads at speed, she would have no option but to career off across the village green. The bumpy ride would finish in the bramble infested hedge at the far side. It would be a bloody and painful end. But not fatal.

The bedraggled victim would stagger home to find a chilling message on her door mat. The Italian had yet to decide which one would be the most appropriate. This together with her accident, should provide a stark message for her to drop her crusade. He emphasised there must be no spectators. It would not be good having people hovering about to watch the crash. The less witnesses the better. Especially when it came to giving police statements.

All the conspirators could do was cross their fingers and nervously await the outcome.

Exactly twenty four hours later they met again. They were greeted by the colonel looking rather edgy.

When all were seated, he explained in grave tones how the plan had gone. The break cable had been successfully cut. And the rider coming down the hill had negotiated the bend. But instead of a headlong ride to the hedge, the journey had ended abruptly. The cricket club had erected its practice nets right in her path. It was the start of the season which nobody had thought about. Like a safety net in a circus, she was caught by them when catapulted into the air. She became heavily entangled. But Norman, the only person passing, had managed to unroll her after a struggle.

The colonel paused. "Before anybody asks Miss Tobias's condition, I must reveal she is very well." He seemed to have difficulty getting his words out. "It was Mavis Pitts on the bike" He waited for the gasps to subside before explaining she normally walked to work. But being late, the missionary had told her to take hers. Unaware of this, Bambini had approached the cottage with his card. He was about to put it through the letter box when Henrietta opened the door. Before he could speak, she told him she did not talk to cold callers and shut it.

There was a long silence. As Arthur said afterwards, you could have heard a bicycle clip drop. But he agreed with everybody else that it was no laughing matter. The professional campaign had begun as disastrously as the amateur. But nobody was blaming the Italian. He had cut the cables efficiently and the rider had done what he expected. Or would have, but for the nets. And who could have allowed for the cleaner being late for work? It was a case of better luck next time. Dame Fortune tended to even herself out and they were due their share. But it had better come quickly. The time for further action was disappearing fast.

Chapter 16

The embarrassing failure made Bambini feel homesick. He didn't mind this cloak and dagger stuff. He was used to it. And there were few better operators. But he preferred a good shoot out. Where bodies were left on the pavement with chalk marks round them. Their blood drying in the hot Italian sun. He conceded that Hatchett was a pretty place. Very pretty. But there was little room for manoeuvre. He could easily slip undetected through the maze of Naples' back streets. Here there were one or two narrow lanes and a main road. And the village was so small it was difficult to get about without bumping into somebody. And then word would spread of a stranger in its midst.

He gave a heartfelt sigh. He had to think clearly. He must plan his next action. And this time nothing must be left to chance. He still did not feel he knew his target well enough, despite all the details on his piece of paper. He had to get inside Henrietta's mind. The deadline was getting nearer, but he would not be hurried. Never mind cleanliness. Thoroughness was next to godliness. More haste less speed. That was his motto. He would shadow her. Slowly and carefully. And then at the right moment, strike. Swift and true. Out of the blue. He liked that. But it would not do for a card. Instinctively, he felt for the cord in his pocket. Only as a last resort, he had promised. He shook his head regretfully.

Chapter 17

"Come in." Ronald Chambers did not bother to get up from behind his desk. He pointed a finger to a chair. "So you have shortened your list of suspects?"

Henrietta sat down carefully. She remembered it was rickety. "No, that is as long as ever. I have come about something different." He raised his eyebrows. "I am being followed and my bicycle is being tampered with." She took a deep breath and went on. "It has been involved in two accidents. Or should I say incidents. In the first an obstacle was placed on a dangerous corner and in the second, the break cables were cut." She elaborated as he sat back, eyes closed. When she had finished, he opened them. "And the shadowing?"

She looked confused.

"You said you are being followed."

"It's just a feeling. I haven't seen anybody yet. I just sense I'm being watched." She gripped the sides of her chair. "But there was one odd occurrence. After the second incident, a strange man came to the door. I shut it before he could speak. I wish now I had asked him what he wanted."

"That might have been a good idea. But perhaps you did the right thing." He clasped his hands in front of him."What do you want me to do?"

"I'm certain this is all connected to my investigation. I want you to find out who is trailing me. And hopefully this will lead to the bottom's owner."

"Maybe they are one and the same person."

"For some reason I don't think so. But I can't put my finger on it. I believe the man who called on me holds the key. I hadn't seen him around before. He seemed kind of foreign. He had a menacing air."

The detective looked at her sombrely. "It could be

your imagination. When people feel persecuted, it can run away with theirs."

Henrietta felt hot under the collar. "I am not imagining anything."

He was unperturbed. "We have to look at all possibilities."

A pleading note came into her voice. "You have to help me."

It was the first time he had seen her appear vulnerable.

"I am fighting on my own at the moment."

"Where is your friend?"

"She got tangled in cricket nets."

He decided not to pursue that line further.

"She has rope burns and broken finger nails," added the visitor. "But she should be fit soon. However I want action now. We must bring this thing to an end."

"If what you say is true, you are up against a considerable number of people."

"God is on my side."

"No, he is on the side of the big battalions."

The missionary's voice regained its edge. "Are you afraid?"

Her listener smiled ruefully. "No. I'm just weighing the odds. You will expect value for your hundred pounds a day. I am not sure I can provide it."

"I am willing to take that risk."

"Well, if you are I am. But don't expect miracles. I know there are plenty in the bible. But this is real life."

Henrietta stood up. "Good. When can you start?"

He scratched the back of his neck. "Tomorrow. I'm not doing anything else."

"Do you want a deposit? I have brought some money with me."

"So you were confident I would come?"

"You do not look like a busy man to me."

"It is true. There are many murders in English villages. But they are nearly all on television." He got to his feet. "Nearly all, but not quite."

She darted a glance at him. "What do you mean?"

"What I say." He escorted her to the door. "I'll take a couple of days in advance. You never know."

"She counted out the notes under his watchful eye. "You're not very good for morale."

He folded them carefully and put them in his pocket. "I deal in facts." He shook her hand. "Now we are two. And when your friend has recovered, we will be three."

Chapter 18

It was a bright, sunny morning as Norman wandered through the village. He did a lot of pottering about. Looking at this and that. His eyes rarely showed more than a flicker of interest beneath his helmet. But he stood transfixed outside the carpentry shop of Harry Pike. The object of his attention was a coffin. It was of fresh pine with silver plated handles. It stood on a long bench with shavings all around it on the floor. Its maker was just positioning the lid. It looked a perfect fit.

Nothing filled the onlooker with horror more than the sight of a coffin. As it would anyone desperate to reach a hundred. But they intrigued him. He found himself in the doorway. "Good morning Mr Pike."

"Good morning Norman."

"Who's it for?"

"Who's what for?"

"That." The speaker could not bring himself to say the word, but pointed to the carpenter's handiwork. Nobody had died in Hatchett. And as far as he knew, nobody was even ill. The figure in his large leather apron, trimmed an edge. "You were a boy scout weren't you Norman?"

"Yes."

"Then you'll know the motto Be Prepared. People pass away all the time. So I'm keeping one ready."

His visitor thought about this. "But nobody's unwell."

"You don't need to be under the weather. Death strikes at any time."

His listener shuddered and turned on his heel. Norman told everybody he met about his gruesome discovery. It did not take long for the whole village to know. The big question was, who had ordered it.?

Those in the conspiracy feared it could only be Bambini. And that its occupant would most certainly be the missionary. It made each of them uneasy. Had it really come to this? And so soon? What about the strict instructions? Was there really going to be a murder in Hatchett?

At the progress meeting that night, the colonel first asked if there were any questions. A forest of hands shot up. Everybody began talking at once. Who was the coffin for? The hubbub brought Ant's wife to the closed door. She caught the distinct reply. It was for Miss Tobias. And long may she lie in it. Holding a hand to her mouth, the eavesdropper hurried off, missing the next sentence. At least, continued the speaker, until she was safe in Italy. There was an array of confused faces. He explained the plan. She would be drugged and transported. There, she would be kept captive in a villa of Ant's relatives until she promised to be sensible.

They all agreed it was a brilliant and humane ploy. Italy was a nice place for a holiday and her keep would be free. Amid the general back slapping, Arthur raised his voice. "How are we going to put her to sleep?"

"It's all organised," replied the colonel reassuringly. "Dr Roberts is taking charge. He will administer his special mixture which will act in seconds. Then she'll be popped into her container and swiftly dispatched. The paperwork will be no problem. Bodies are transported to their final resting places all the time. He has all the necessary forms."

"But how will he stick in the needle?" persisted the newsagent.

"That is still being considered," admitted the military figure. "We did think of a flu jab for all the village. But that wouldn't work in early June."

"What about one of those blow pipes?" chipped in the landlord. "You know, the ones they use in South

American jungles. Then you wouldn't have to get too close."

A look if irritation crossed the colonel's features. "I don't think they're readily available in Hatchett."

"Well, vets use tranquilliser guns," proclaimed the reverend. "There should be plenty of those about."

"But you have to chose your spot," said constable Tompkins. "We don't want her toppling over in public."

The colonel called for silence. "This is getting out of hand," he declared. "I will pass you over to George."

The doctor adjusted his cuffs. "We are not after a runaway bull," he said. "And I am not looking for a posse. Everybody has become over excited. It involves one simple injection. And as a general practitioner, I am well qualified to give it."

"But you'll never get her in range if she knows what it's for," protested Arthur.

"There are plenty of ways to bring a patient into the surgery," he replied evenly. "And my job will be made much simpler if you all carried on as if nothing was happening."

This was easier said than done. The atmosphere was tense. Everybody was willing the venture to succeed. If it failed like the rest, what then? Ant had said his cousin never aborted a mission. And as each day passed, there would be fewer options.

That night Rosa could not sleep. She endlessly tossed and turned. Ant lay like a log beside her. Had her ears played her tricks? No, they had not. It was unmistakable. Miss Tobias was to be killed. She and her husband might not be plunging in the knife. But the victim's end had been plotted in their home. And Antonio, being at the meeting, was an accessory. What if he was arrested? She could not run the restaurant on her own. Her face grimaced in the darkness. But there would be no death. She would warn Henrietta. It was the only thing to do. And fair. After all, it was the missionary who had told her about the sports dinner when everybody else was trying to keep it a secret. First thing in the morning she would repay that debt. Her mind made up, she finally dropped off. In one dream Antonio was slipping out of the premises carrying his butcher's knife. But when she awoke, he was snoring beside her.

Flinging on her clothes at first light, Rosa tiptoed downstairs. Stopping only to lift the cat off the fruit bowl, she let herself out of the back door. It was a fresh morning. She shivered. And not just from the cold. It would be quite a shock for Henrietta. What if she fainted? The bearer of bad news was not good at slapping faces to bring people round. At least Mavis Pitts would be there. So if the victim needed to be lifted up, the cleaner could take one end.

Yet Miss Tobias proved to be of sterner stuff. Her eyes glittered. She felt God sitting on her shoulder. She was her grandfather in the jungle. No, that wouldn't do. He was eaten. But she would be far too tough for them to sink their teeth into. And they had to catch her first. She forced herself to stay calm. Hatchett might be a den of iniquity, but it was still an English village. There would be no tom toms beating. Well, not ones you could hear. At least she would not be cut down in the street. She would just have to avoid dangerous places. She ran through them. The newsagents, the church, the convent, the restaurant, the pub. She frowned. That did not leave much. Should she go away for the last few days before giving her evidence? Her expression became resolute. No, she would not be driven out of town. And anyway, she was not alone. Her band was growing. Ronald Chambers was due any minute. Mavis was downstairs and nearly fully recovered. And now Rosa had joined. Was there anybody else who could come to her aid? She shook her head sadly. She had to face facts. Hatchett was full of reprobates.

Ant's wife was holding the missionary's hand as if she was the one needing support. Her mind was in turmoil. She loved her husband and had always been loyal. Yet she had betrayed him. Or had she? Maybe she was saving him from himself. But now the step had been taken, she would stay the course. She would do whatever she could to help Miss Tobias stay alive. She looked at her watch. She had to go. But she could be counted upon. As she left the detective arrived. He raised his ancient trilby to her as they passed on the path. Fellow gang members as they were soon to become.

Henrietta heaved a sigh of relief at the sight of her rotund ally. He might not look much, but she did not doubt his skill at the tricks of his trade. And they were sure to be needed. He asked for a large cup of black coffee. It was always his way to start the day. Particularly if it was going to be a long one. As he was certain the next few would be. She wasted no time in bringing him up to date.

"They are trying to kill me," she said calmly.

As always, he wanted to know the facts. "How do you know?"

"The restaurateur's wife just told me."

"How does she know?"

"She overheard them plotting."

"Who are they'?"

"The conspirators."

"How many?"

"Nearly everybody in the village."

He put down his cup. "Well, what did she say?"

Henrietta told him word for word as she had been told word for word.

He frowned. "Where was she when she heard this?"

"She had her ear to the door"

Typical woman, he thought. He pulled tentatively at an ear lobe. "Are you sure the coffin exists?"

The missionary was most decisive. "Oh yes. Lots of people have seen it. It's in Mr Pike's carpentry shop. He made it."

The detective was thoughtful. "If they want to murder you, why do they need a coffin? They would just bury you in the ground. Coffins are for transporting."

"Maybe they don't want to leave the evidence lying around the village."

"Maybe, but it doesn't really add up."

"What are you going to do?"

"I don't know yet. First we must consider going to the police."

"I thought of that. But it's not good telling constable Tompkins. He's in with them."

"What about officers in the next town?"

"I don't think they would believe me."

"He nodded. "That could be a problem."

She stared at him. "Do you believe me?"

"Given the background to everything, on balance I do." He rubbed his chin. "But of course that's all hearsay. The police would need something concrete."

"Like a coffin?"

"Yes, but it is not yours until you are in it. Or rather put in it."

Henrietta shuddered. "You don't have to labour the point."

"Well, it hasn't come to that yet. I will have a sniff around Hatchett. But as a stranger, people are not likely to talk to me. Yet something might come up."

He rose to go as Mavis burst in. "I saw Rosa leaving. What did she want?"

The missionary's face was grave. "She came to tell

me I am to be killed." She waved her hand towards her companion. "Do you remember Mr Chambers? He is trying to keep me alive."

The detective was buttoning his coat. "Yes, among other duties. It's nice to see you again Miss Pitts."

"You are lucky to," rejoined Henrietta. "She was on my bike when the breaks failed. It was meant to be me. She was saved by those cricket nets I mentioned. Otherwise she could have been really badly hurt."

He looked at her quizzically. "Are you sure it wasn't a maintenance problem?"

"Definitely. The cables were cut clean as a whistle."

"I'm still sore," added the cleaner. "And still sore at the person who did it."

The detective was suddenly alert. "Where was the bike?"

"Right outside my door," said the intended victim. "Whoever it was acted quickly and quietly. A very efficient operation."

"That doesn't sound like a local. Are there any newcomers about?"

"Not really. I think Ant at the restaurant has a cousin staying with him. But he keeps himself out of the way. Nobody sees him."

"Ant? That's a funny name."

"It's short for Antonio."

"So he's Italian?"

"I suppose he must be. He looks like one."

"Then his cousin comes from Italy?"

Henrietta nodded. "Naples apparently."

"What does he look like?"

"As I said, I haven't see him."

"Don't you think it's odd that a man comes on holiday and remains invisible?"

"Maybe he likes a quiet life."

"Or maybe he has a reason for trying not to be

noticed."

"Like cutting cables." broke in Mavis.

"Exactly."

The missionary looked astonished. "But why would he want to do that? He's a stranger."

Mr Chambers kept his voice calm. "But he is connected to Ant who owns the premises where the plan to murder you was discussed."

There was a long silence. Miss Tobias finally broke it. "You mean he was brought over here deliberately?"

"It is possible. He may be a professional in that sort of business. The locals would want to keep their hands clean."

Henrietta was thinking hard. "What sort of business?"

"The sort the Italians are good at."

"Rubbing people out," intervened Mavis.

The missionary put a hand to her mouth. "That man at the door. The one I wouldn't talk to. He came on the day of the accident. He was foreign looking. Could it have been Ant's cousin?"

"A definite possibility," replied the detective who was beginning to feel a hundred pounds a day was chicken feed. "What we need," he said, "is to get a better look at him. I believe he has been brought here to frighten you off. But things have started to get out of control. Having failed so far, they are upping the stakes."

"What should I do?"

"You have two choices. You can barricade yourself in here or go about as if nothing is happening. I think you should carry on. Nobody is going to murder you in broad daylight. And it may draw the conspirators out into the open. We must not forget your original quest. To find the owner of that mysterious bottom. He is obviously very involved in the plot."

Henrietta sighed. "And all because I looked over that convent wall." She brightened. "But God made me do it. I am his instrument. And you are both his disciples."

The detective looked out of the window. "I wouldn't go as far as to say that."

"But you are," she exclaimed. "You have chosen the path of righteousness. Blessed are they who do the Lord's work."

Mr Chambers was already across the room. He stopped in the doorway and held up a little black book. It bulged with phone numbers. "This is my bible," he declared, and was gone.

Chapter 19

Arthur and Angela Broad stood sorrowfully by the coffin. Mr Pike had refused their request.

"It would have been just right for our new vampire film," the newsagent lamented.

"I am sorry," said its maker. "I have strict instructions to take it to the doctor's surgery. It might be needed at any moment."

"But we only want it for twenty four hours. Our cardboard one collapsed when Angela rested her breasts on it."

"I can't help that."

"We'll mention your shop in the credits."

"That is one advertisement I can do without."

Angela looked at the coveted object's sleek lines. "It's a fine piece of work."

The carpenter nodded. "It is that. And it's for a worthy cause. Miss Tobias will find it comfortable to travel in."

"It looks a good fit," agreed Arthur.

"It is. The reverend gave me her measurements after her fitting for a choir gown. She'll be nice and snug. No rolling about."

"We've got to sedate her first," said Angela anxiously.

Mr Pike picked up his wooden mallet. "I'd creep up behind her with this. It's the simplest way. But I've no doubt the doctor will do the job." He paused. "I've heard it just takes one prick. And then out like a light. I wonder what she'll feel like waking up in a strange country."

"And no doubt with a thumping headache," added the newsagent.

"She'll feel lucky to be alive," declared his wife with

conviction. "Not many people get out of a coffin." She shuddered as she pictured it. What if Miss Tobias suffered from claustrophobia like she did? Well it wouldn't matter. she'd be unconscious. The doctor would know the right amount of drug to give for the journey. But what if the plane was delayed? She'd wake up in the confined darkness and scream. Then the airport staff would come running. She hastily repelled the image. She'd made too many home movies. She wasn't fond of the missionary. Far from it. But she didn't want that to happen.

The couple stepped out into the evening sunlight and set off for their shop. Gavin was due soon. It was time for their latest epic The Voluptuous Vampire. Using a proper coffin would have been nice, mused Angela. But she had to admit it would have been a tight squeeze. Nature had been kind to her. But being 48-23-36 had its drawbacks.

Not long after they left, Bambini appeared. He ran his fingers along the beautifully finished pine. It felt good, very good. An excellent job all round. He smiled appreciatively at Mr Pike. One day it would be used for a proper funeral. Maybe even his own. It was a bit long for him. But he wanted to be buried with his dear departed cat which he kept in his deep freeze. There would be room for both of them. He came to with a start. He had forgotten to say goodbye to Toni. He always lifted the lid and winked at his pet lying amid the frozen ravioli. Ant's cousin was superstitious. He felt a flicker of anxiety. He had broken his routine. It was rushing to the printers on the way to the airport which had thrown him out. Would his mission now end badly? He had never failed before.

He sensed Mr Pike watching him intently. He pulled himself together and gave the carpenter another smile. Of course everything was all right. His plan was brilliant. And the vital equipment for carrying it out was standing before him. All it needed now was its occupant. He helped its maker load it onto a trolley. Then, one pushing and the other pulling, they made their way up the deserted street towards the surgery. Its squeaking wheels hid the sound of shuffling footsteps twenty yards behind. Ronald Chambers was stiff after spending an hour crouched behind the little war memorial. But it had given him a perfect view of the carpenter's shop. Now there was an eager air about him as he followed the coffin to its destination.

It was ten o'clock when the detective arrived at the missionary's cottage. He was right, It had been a long day. But not unproductive. He had discovered where her intended accommodation was being kept. And was certain that despite the gathering gloom, one of its escorts was the mysterious Italian. From his description, Henrietta agreed it was the sinister man who had knocked on her door. Appearances could prove deceptive. But one thing was clear. If he was associated with the coffin, he was up to no good. And anyway, why was it being kept in the surgery? The doctor must be in the plot too. Her companion could only agree. If they weren't going to do away with her secretly, he would be on hand to give an innocent cause of death and sign the certificate.

The conversation was giving Henrietta the creeps. And the wind outside rattling the windows did not help. Although it was not a cold night, she shivered. The detective gave her a sympathetic glance. She might be a tough old bird but her predicament would give anyone the willies. He got to his feet. He needed a good sleep but would be back in the morning. She said she hoped she would be there to greet him.

Chapter 20

Constable Tompkins wallowed in the bath. His girth meant his stomach protruded out of the water. It was a pink island. He placed the soap on top. It would be easier to reach. If only the other things in life were as easy. Getting rid of Miss Tobias was going to be tricky. Especially if she just vanished. People disappeared all the time, often without fuss. But if inquiries were made, it could be awkward. It all depended on if it created any interest. As far as he knew, she had no relatives. But she was quite close to that cleaner woman. What if she started to ask questions? As the officer on the spot, he would have to lead any investigation. He could hardly bump her off as well. That's what occurred in films. You had to keep silencing people to keep the lid on. But if that happened, there'd be nobody left in the village. He would just have to keep his fingers crossed that everything would go perfectly. Yet that rarely happened in Hatchett. And certainly not since Miss Tobias had arrived. He looked at his bruises which were now a faint yellow. He wondered just how fast the bicycle was going when it hit him. At least this time he would be on the sidelines when the action took place. If it did. He was puzzling like the others over how the doctor would stick the needle in.

At that moment, George was thinking exactly the same thing. He was still working on how to get her into the surgery. It was looking more difficult than it had at first appeared. He sat at his desk wearing a concerned expression. What were the other options? If any. He recalled the Bulgarian dissident who was killed by a poisoned umbrella tip at a London bus stop. He could hardly jab the missionary with one. And anyway, it hadn't rained for weeks. He studied a tobacco stained finger. Must get the pumice stone on to that, he thought. It's setting a bad example. His mind was continuing to work hard. When would she be at her the most vulnerable? With her guard down? His eyes lit up. Of course, in church. But could he get close to her? He was not a regular worshipper and could not see himself joining the choir. Anyway, it was too late for that.

There was nothing else for it. The vicar would have to do it. He would give him lessons. It was easy, but you had to get it right first time. And at the end of the service. The fewer people aware of what was happening the better. They would think she had merely fainted. Ronnie would catch her. and the colonel would be there to help. He sat in the front pew. The pair would carry her out of the side door. Then it was just two hundred yards to the surgery. And plop, into the coffin she'd go, The air holes would be checked, the lid screwed down and all would be ready. The landlord would take it to Heathrow in his van. Bambini would accompany it as a grieving relative. He was good around coffins. At the other end, once clear of the airport, he would whip out his screw driver to let in the fresh air. Then its occupant would slowly come round.

The doctor could see no reason why everything should not go to plan. Though he had to admit, there was a slight worry about the vicar's shaky hand. Members of the congregation taking the sacrament, had often to anticipate sudden changes of direction.

The doctor lost no time in asking the assassin as he called him, over for a cup of tea. Although it was said fondly and was not strictly true, his visitor thought it an unfortunate word. He sat opposite his host nervously fingering his dog collar. At the original conspirators' meeting, everybody had pledged to stand up and be counted. And to undertake any little task to ensure the success of the operation. The man of God had meant it most sincerely. As they all had. But now his time had come, he was less sure. It was all very well for George to call it 'just a little jab.' He was not the one having to do it. It might be a piece of cake to him. He had done thousands of them. But his stand-in would have to rely on beginner's luck. What if he missed? What if she saw the syringe? And what a place to do it in. The Lord's house.

The most important thing said George, was to get the feel of the instrument. Light as a feather and easy to handle. Then to practice squeezing out its contents. Not too slow, not too fast. Just gentle constant pressure. Picking one from a cabinet behind him, he filled it with water. Then deftly injected the soft arm of his chair before handing the needle to the vicar. The new recruit followed suit. The doctor was right. There was nothing to it. Admittedly it was only foam and not the missionary. But its texture was almost the same as human flesh. His confidence began to grow. Maybe it was not so difficult after all.

The pair decided it was time to put their plan of action to Bambini. He was the mastermind who had the final say. They were as excited as schoolboys as they entered the back door of the restaurant. Ant's cousin was sitting at the kitchen table in shirt sleeves and sporting a pair of red braces. He listened to them in silence. He just managed to stop his lip from curling, but could not hide the note of contempt in his voice. He had never heard anything so stupid. He vetoed it immediately. For a start, there would be far too many witnesses. There had to be as few onlookers as possible. And the perpetrator had to be coolly professional. The vicar was more used to holding a prayer book than a needle. He was just as likely to inject himself. The object of this assessment felt a surge of relief mixed with indignation. He had nerved himself after his practice session to take up the challenge. But as the bible said, many are called but few are chosen.

So what did Bambini think? The Italian had let the doctor organise the operation but had feared it would come to this. So he had been considering his own options. His preference was for a bullet behind the ear. But of course that had to be ruled out. Yet he knew the best chance of success called for a direct attack. That meant knocking on her door and seizing her as she opened it. Then swiftly sticking in the needle. It would take three of them. One each side to pin her arms. And another in the middle to do the jabbing. They would have to act with the cleaner out of the way. There must be no witnesses. And it would be for Mavis's own safety. If it was dark and the adrenalin flowing, there could be the risk of mistaken identity. And that would be unfair after she'd already been thrown from the bike. But there must be no more beating about the bush, declared the mastermind, selecting one of his few English phrases. Henrietta was due to tell all to the Mother Superior in three days. They would strike that night.

It was perfect timing. Mavis was due to sweep the church after evensong and the vicar knew she would be absent until ten o'clock.

At nine thirty, the trio gathered in the shadow of nearby trees. Ronnie and the general practitioner donned balaclavas at the cottage gate. There was no need to be recognised unnecessarily. The Italian wore a black wide brimmed hat pulled down over his bristly countenance. The collar of his overcoat was turned up. In his right hand was an imitation pistol carved from a lump of wood by the carpenter. His other was left free to do the knocking. He would go first. He hoped his menacing appearance would leave their victim rooted to the spot in sheer fright. He and the vicar would grip her arms while the doctor swiftly did the business. A wind had got up to shake the branches on the trees opposite. These danced about in a blackened sky. There could hardly be better conditions. And so it proved. The missionary thought it was Mavis returning early and had forgotten her key. She opened the door with a smile to be confronted by a most terrifying figure. It raised a gun to her head. "Goodbye," it said in a soft, guttural voice.

Henrietta was made of stern stuff. But the shock was complete. She went into a dead faint. Bambini's practiced hands caught her before she hit the floor. The doctor brought out his syringe while the vicar produced a torch. Then under its slightly wavering beam, the deed was done. In one movement, the Italian lifted the limp body over his shoulder. Being taller than her carrier, the missionary's hands and legs dangled dangerously close to the ground. But he strode out purposefully for the surgery with the others hurrying in his wake. It was a short journey and they met nobody at that hour. The coffin was waiting with its lid off. The victim was laid carefully inside. The doctor checked her pulse and breathing. All was as it should be. She would be collected by the landlord and Bambini at eight in the morning. A midday flight had already been booked. By this time tomorrow she would be safely out of the way in her new home.

Everything worked like clockwork. There were no delays on the motorway and the plane left on time. Bambini rang to say they had landed. He would call again when opening the coffin clear of the city. Hatchett was suddenly a cheerful place once more. People had a spring in their step. Now there would be nobody poking their nose into their affairs. It was as if a heavy cloud had been lifted. Ant had organised early evening drinks at his restaurant for his fellow conspirators. There could hardly have been a happier atmosphere. There was a full turn out with speeches of congratulation and much hearty back slapping. They imagined Henrietta waking up with a thumping headache. They didn't wish her more harm than that. But she had provided enough of them herself with her prying and running to the authorities. The partygoers were magnanimous. She would be welcomed back when she promised to stop her antics. And a brush with the mafia should certainly help her come to her senses.

Ant took his cousin's next call. The colour drained from his face. His free hand held the edge of the nearest table for support. "Rocks" he said to the startled onlookers. "It's full of rocks."

"What is?" asked Angela.

"The coffin. It's full of rocks."

"It can't be," said constable Tompkins. "There wouldn't be room for her."

"Instead of," explained the colonel who was quick on the uptake. "Somebody has done a swap."

"Well, if she's not in it, where is she?" said the landlord.

"With whoever swapped her," replied the military figure.

But nobody among the shocked gathering had any idea who it could be.

Chapter 21

Mavis had returned that night to find the cottage empty. She was not at first worried. Henrietta liked a little late evening snooping. But on the other hand she had promised they would have a cocoa together. And her coat was hanging up in the hall. It was not that chilly, but she would have worn it to go out. The cleaner was wondering what to do when there came an unexpected tap on the door. To her great relief it was Mr Chambers. He might look scruffy, but he had a reassuring air about him. And this time a satisfied one as well. He had just come from burgling the convent. And in the office had discovered an interesting accounts book. At least he believed that's what it was. Could he discuss it was Miss Tobias? No he could not. She had disappeared. A picture of a coffin came into his head. Followed by one of the surgery. He realised where she was likely to be.

"Come on," he urged, taking her arm. "We have no time to lose."

The two figures hurried through the darkness. It was pitch black. The moon was tucked behind the clouds. The detective flashed his torch through the letterbox. The coffin lay in the hall. It took him less than two minutes to pick the lock. Was Henrietta inside? He felt under its rim and found what he was looking for. Air holes. She most certainly was. Selecting a screwdriver from several in his pocket, he took off the lid. The missionary's pale face stared up at him. She was breathing evenly, her hands clasped in front of her as if in prayer. He sent Mavis to search the undergrowth across the road for large stones. Enough to match the victim's weight. Better to let the kidnappers think their plot had succeeded rather than have a hue and cry in the morning. Gingerly he lifted her out and laid her on the carpet. Then he went to help his companion. With the proceeds of their hunt safely inside he added earth to stop them rolling. Then he carefully screwed down the lid. Together, as gently as possible, they carried the missionary back to the cottage. They both felt it was unwise for her to stay there. So they transferred her to the back seat of the detective's car. Then with her head cradled in Mavis's lap, he drove the pair to his flat in the nearby town.

The doctor's dose had been expertly calculated. It was not until the next evening that Henrietta began to regain consciousness. The first thing she saw was the concerned faces of her rescuers. They swam in and out of view as they hovered above her. She had a nasty headache and her arms and legs felt numb. She was lying on the sofa in the lounge. She tried to get up but nothing seemed to work. She felt like a wooden doll. The inside of her mouth tasted of sawdust. She gratefully sipped from the glass of water Mavis held to her lips. Gradually the room came into focus. It danced around a little but then settled down. Finally she found her voice. "Where am I?" It was barely above a whisper.

"You are safe in my flat," replied the detective. "But you have had quite an adventure."

Miss Tobias managed to sit up. With two pillows to support her back, she told her listeners the last thing she remembered. That sinister figure holding a gun to her head. She was sure she was going to die. Then everything went black. While Mavis dampened her forehead with a wet flannel, Donald Chambers explained how they had found her and covered up her rescue.

She looked perplexed. "Where were they taking me?"

He shrugged his shoulders. "Who knows for certain.

But far enough away to stop you exposing the convent and prying into Hatchett's affairs." He looked at her exhausted face. "Judging by the amount of dope they gave you, it must have been a fair distance. And as that Italian appears involved, I would hazard a guess and say Italy."

She put a hand to her head. "But what then?"

"They would have kept you captive until you agreed to call off your investigations."

She painfully shook her head as her strength began to return. "Never."

"You might feel differently if you were in a strange land," said Mavis. "You have had a lucky escape."

"Yes, thanks to you two. You saved me with God's help. I know he wants me to continue. I will most definitely attend the meeting with the mother superior."

The detective felt in his pocket. "I have some more ammunition for you." He pulled out a sheet of paper. "I visited the convent while you were being kidnapped. Everyone was at prayers so I had the office to myself. I found a little black book with dates, times and initials. Unfortunately none match the names of anyone in Hatchett. Whoever kept the record intended it to remain secret. If the rumours of double accounting are true, there will be an official book with the real people and the payments they were supposedly given. All we would have to do is match them up." He felt the missionary's eyes upon him. "I ran out of time before I could find the second one."

Mavis looked on the bright side. "At least we have this information. Even if we can't yet decipher it. That is a step forward."

Henrietta made herself more comfortable. "What exactly is written down?"

"On the date you peered over the wall, two visitors appear to be in the frame. One was there between two twenty and two fifty five. And the other from three ten until three thirty."

"And how are they identified?"

"With the letters K.K. and S.S. It is obviously some sort of code."

"They may not necessarily refer to people," said Mavis.

"What are you getting at?" said the detective.

They could be describing the prowess of the visitors."

The missionary's face clouded. "I don't understand."

"K.K. could be a King Kong performance. You know, marks out of ten." The equivalent on her honeymoon had been three.

Henrietta's eyes flashed. "I've never heard anything so stupid."

Yet Donald Chambers thought there might be something in it. "That is not an uncommon thing for lovers to do," he declared. "What about S.S?"

The cleaner thought hard. "So, so."

He nodded. "Could be." He paused. "Then that points to K.K. being the culprit."

The missionary leaned forward. "What do you mean?"

"The performance you so vividly describe is unlikely to be rated so, so."

"I agree," said Mavis.

Miss Tobias had fully come to her senses and felt her frustration rising. "This is quite ridiculous. We have no idea what the letters stand for."

"Maybe," said the detective. "But we have to examine all possibilities. Sometimes the most unexpected proves to be true."

"It is time now to leave everything to the Mother Superior. She will demand answers and all will be revealed."

"It will certainly be an interesting few days," he replied. "There will be a lot of people feeling the pressure in Hatchett."

"I still say it's King Kong," said Mavis looking out of the window. Her own husband had been more like a chimpanzee. It was just as well that he had run off.

Chapter 22

Bambini stared at the empty coffin. Empty that is of its occupant. He fingered the rocks. He wanted to strangle each individually. Opening the car window, he hurled them one by one into the roadside ditch. He hoped the exertion would calm him. But he felt the blood pumping round his body faster than ever. It was too dangerous to continue his journey. He would ram the first vehicle he came across. And then run over its occupants. He put his head in his hands. What was happening? He was the ice cold assassin. Yet he was shaking with rage. He had been outwitted by a missionary. And a female one at that. What if word reached his mafia friends? He felt sick. No it must not. That would be the end. His brain cleared. He would return to England immediately to finish the job. Revenge was a dish best taken cold. But he could not wait for that. And this time there would be no wishy washy thinking. He would get a real gun. He had the contacts in London. And then it would be his favourite spot behind the ear. As it should have been in the first place. Then they would not be in this mess. There must be no interference.

He looked puzzled. But how had she got out? She had appeared to be deeply drugged. The doctor had done his calculations most carefully. Bambini had seen to that. He didn't want her hammering on the lid going through customs. And the top had been firmly screwed down. He had made sure of it himself. There was only one answer. She had been rescued. But by whom? According to his cousin, she had been ostracized by the entire village. Apart from that little woman she lived with. And she hadn't seemed up to much. He thought hard. Was somebody playing a double game? The

English appeared to be civilised. But he wouldn't put it past them. Never trust anyone, his grandmother always said. And it invariably turned out to be true. He had looked upon his victims as ciphers or numbers. There had never been anything personal.

But now there was. Henrietta had roused his fury. She would be mercilessly rubbed out. And although he knew he would be in control of himself by then, he would use several bullets. Just for the satisfaction. Or what about his trusty cord? He put his hand in his pocket to feel the familiar friend. He would weigh up the pros and cons on the plane. It would depend a lot on circumstances. But either would do very nicely. He took several deep breaths. He felt calmer now. He would return to his flat for a quick shower and change of clothes. And before leaving, he would open the freezer and wink at Toni. Attention to detail. That's what counted. That's what had let him down last time.

Back in England, the colonel was rapping on the table. "Ant has called this emergency meeting so I will hand over straight away to him."

The restaurateur exuded a very sombre air. As well he might with the news he had to impart. "I have had an urgent call from my aunt Maria in Naples," he began. "Bambini is on his way back" He paused. "To murder the missionary."

There were startled looks around the room followed by much gasping.

"He told her that?" asked Arthur."

"No, he never said a word to her. He didn't need to. She knows his look when he sets off to kill. His eyes go deadly cold. You can almost see the ice forming round the pupils."

"But what's the point?" said the landlord. "We don't know where she is. And by the time he arrives, it will be too late anyway. She will have told everything to the

Mother Superior."

Ant gave a short laugh. "It is revenge, pure and simple. It is the mafia's best reason."

The vicar put into words what everybody was thinking. "But why does she have to die for escaping from a coffin?"

The Italian rolled his eyes at his naivety. "She has ruined his reputation. I have seen his CV. She will be an ugly blot on it. Before it was a hundred percent, never a botched job." He launched into his explanation. "He kills in three ways. His weapons are the cord, the knife and the gun. With the first, the victim is dead after one gurgle. Although if he is in a mood to listen, he will allow two or three. He likes the blade the least. It is messy. He always wipes it afterwards on his tie. A row of these blood stained mementoes hang in his wardrobe. With the third, it is a bullet into the back of the ear. He is not fussy. It does not matter which one."

Several of his listeners shifted uneasily. They had never heard Bambini described in such deadly fashion. They had thought of him as a frightener rather than a killer. The vicar's scruples were coming to the surface. "We cannot let him murder her."

"But how can we prevent it?" asked Angela.

"That's the point," declared Ant. "We can't. He is now like a robot. If we all knelt down before him pleading for mercy, he would fire a shot over our heads to bring us to our senses. There will be no interference. Nothing will be allowed to stand in his way. He will track her down. And then -"

"And then what?" said the newsagent.

"He will strike as swiftly as a snake." There was a collective shudder from his audience as he continued. "He will carry one other item. A delayed action camera. With revenge killings he loves to photograph himself by the body. A hunter with its prey. He hangs the pictures on his wall. The last time I visited, there were six."

"Let's be pragmatic about this," said the landlord calmly. "It's her own fault for getting out of the coffin."

"She didn't get out," corrected the doctor huffily. "She was lifted out. She was unconscious. I gave her the exact dose. Right down to the last grain."

"All right, lifted out. But it must have been a terrible shock to Bambini. Finding those rocks."

"But who did the lifting?" asked PC 42 whose investigative instincts were not quite extinguished.

"That is immaterial," replied James, irritated at being side tracked.

"No, it's not. Because whoever it was is probably guarding her."

"So they could be in danger too," added the colonel with his military thinking.

"There will be no massacre," said Ant in his most reassuring tone. "But it is interesting who has got her. Yes?"

There were several nods of agreement.

"She's not in the cottage as far as we can tell," said the vicar. "But neither is the cleaner. So they must be somewhere together."

"But she couldn't have got Miss Tobias out on her own," exclaimed the doctor, still miffed at her escape.

"That's right," agreed the landlord. "If she'd tried to carry her off, her legs would have trailed on the ground. There were no marks to be found."

"But what about that stranger seen snooping about?" asked Arthur. "The small man with a moustache."

"He was seen at the cottage," chipped in his wife

"A travelling salesman," said the landlord knowledgably. "I know the type."

"What?" she replied. "At ten o'clock at night?"

The colonel perked up. "When was this?"

"Two evenings ago. That was the one she disappeared on."

The doctor's voice betrayed a tremor. "Then maybe there is a connection. If he's an outsider, she must have hired him."

"A mercenary," said the colonel. "She is increasing her forces."

"They're not as big as ours," declared the newsagent defiantly.

"Agreed. But we're a rabble. Three successive missions have ended in disaster."

"It's true," admitted the vicar. "And now we've lost the war. Henrietta's seeing the Mother Superior tomorrow."

Sister Martina attended every meeting. But usually she kept quiet. She saw her role mainly as an observer. But she could not contain herself at this abject surrender. "You should be ashamed of yourself," she cried. "It's just as well Winston Churchill cannot hear you." Typical protestant, she thought. About as much use in a fight as a paper bag. And speaking of paper bags, she would need one to be sick in if this attitude persisted. She appealed to the colonel for support. "Can't we re-marshall our forces?"

"We can try. What do you have in mind?"

"The village has to defend the convent. The Mother Superior will be down here breathing holy fire. And I and my entire flock could be cast into the wilderness."

"If she is truly of the Lord," said Ronnie. "She will find it in her heart to forgive your sins. I suggest a fulsome apology will do."

Sister Martina shook her head. "Sackcloth and ashes won't work. I know her. She's the old testament kind. Even her finger nails will be sharpened."

The colonel beside her, tried to restore calm. "What we need is a plan. Nothing works without one."

"And where we're concerned," said Arthur, "nothing works with one."

The military figure gave him a severe look. "This is no time for levity. We have to rally behind Sister Martina."

"Exactly," replied the object of this remark. "We must make the Mother Superior realise she is taking on the whole village as well. And of course, Hatchett is in the firing line. Miss Tobias claims to know the identity of my miscreant nun. If our inquisitor gets her hands on her all will be revealed." She looked round the table. "I am aware there are several hearts in this room beating a little faster. And there will be more further afield. My top priority is to keep the girl out of the way. I have considered everything from sending her on a pilgrimage to heavily sedating her and hiding her in a cupboard. But I have yet to come up with a satisfactory solution."

"Maybe she could meet with an accident," ventured the landlord.

"We've had enough of those," the colonel replied sharply.

"No, sorry. I meant incident. She could claim to have seen a ghost. To be struck dumb with terror. You know, lost her voice."

"Look," said Sister Martina with exasperation. "Can we be serious."

"I was only trying to help," James said defensively.

"Maybe it would be better if you were struck dumb," said the newsagent.

"Order. order," shouted the colonel, banging on the tablecloth with the end of a knife. "This is ridiculous. We must keep our minds on our task."

"Or rather tasks," remarked the doctor gravely. "We have to stop Bambini killing the missionary. Otherwise her death will be on all our consciences. And we have to stop the Mother Superior from interrogating you know who. Otherwise several of Hatchett's most respectable inhabitants will be caught with their trousers down. This would be most unfortunate. Especially for the one who exposed his rear to public view."

"Succinctly put," said their military leader as he eyed each of them in turn. "So once more, what are we going to do about it?"

There was a long silence broken only by general fidgeting. It was difficult to sit still when action was urgently needed. But nobody had any idea what.

Chapter 23

Henrietta read her statement through for the third time. Ten densely packed pages in her neat copperplate style. There were slight squiggles where she came to the part of looking over the wall. Several weeks after the event, her emotions still ran high and made her hand shake. She knew the Mother Superior would grill her. But she wanted the record down in black and white. Every spit and cough, as the crude expression went.

Mr Chambers drove. Mavis went along too to give her support. The women sat together in the back of his elderly saloon watching the countryside speed by. The missionary was lost in thought. Had she left anything out? No, except for the identity of constable Marrow as she had promised. She owed him that. He had provided the nun's name. That was the key. That was the breakthrough. She was nearing the end of this particular quest. But once the convent was sorted out, she would not neglect the village. Oh no. Who for instance, had put her in the coffin? She highly suspected the doctor was one of them. He would have administered the drug. And what about that little matter of the LSD? What had been behind that? And then there was that menacing, mystery figure who'd helped kidnap her. The last thing she had seen before blacking out. Yet she had sensed there were three waiting to pounce. So who was the third hovering in the darkness? She realised with dismay it could have been almost anyone. Such were the forces arrayed against her.

But however great they were, she would triumph. And why? Because in all her trials, God was sitting on her shoulder. He would guide her safely through her task. She quaked at the size of it. There was only one way to describe Hatchett. It was a mixture of Sodom and Gomorrah albeit with a pinch of Budleigh Salterton.

The car swept up the drive of the Mother Superior's residence. It was a large house made of local yellow stone surrounded by neatly trimmed lawns. The detective and cleaner remained in their seats. All they could do now was wish the avenging angel good luck.

The Mother Superior was waiting in the drawing room. She glided noiselessly across the carpet to greet her guest. Her handshake was firm. As was Henrietta's. Ten bony fingers and thumbs clasped together in a tight ball. A sledgehammer for justice. The pair were almost the same height, although the missionary's long neck made her look taller. Her hostess's angular features were set in grim lines. Not against her visitor, but at the tidings she brought. The Mother Superior to her credit, admitted that at first she had been suspicious of Henrietta's intentions. Having heard of her background, she feared it was a protestant plot to discredit the convent. But now they had met, she could see God's righteousness flowing through her. And she was further put at ease to learn that the Anglican church had been up to its tricks too. And that Miss Tobias had come down on it with an equal number of bricks. Metaphorically speaking they must number hundreds of thousands. Hatchett indeed was a den of iniquity.

The pillars of their twin faiths sat in armchairs either side of an open fireplace. There was no fire. It was summer. But flames were leaping high in their respective breasts. A plate of biscuits lay untouched between them. Henrietta had been brought up not to talk with her mouth full. And if she had stopped to munch, the tension would have been unbearable. The Mother Superior hung on her every word. She was leaning so far forward, she was almost touching her guest's knee. Her stern countenance had softened a little. She felt a stab of sympathy for her. Those eyes which had seen the glory of the coming of the Lord, had then witnessed a devastating spectacle. But the listener's brain was sharp and clear. She had not been made a Mother Superior for nothing. Each assertion must be checked as far as humanly possible. She took a deep breath and posed her first question. "Was it hairy?"

Henrietta frowned momentarily. "Was what hairy?"

"The naked flesh in question."

"Surely that's immaterial."

"No, I'm afraid it's not." The speaker continued warily. "This is very distasteful but has to be said. It is sadly a fact in convents that some nuns er, prefer each others company. What I am saying is, it might have been two of them rather than one being a male. That of course would be equally dreadful. But it would alter the situation."

The missionary's reply was adamant. "It was definitely a man's behind."

Her companion picked her words carefully. "You have seen many of these?"

Her visitor coloured. "No."

"Then how do you know?"

"I just do. It was sort of the way it was acting."

The Mother Superior felt there was no need to go further in this direction. She nodded sombrely. "Then we will leave it at that."

"And there is another reason I am coming to," said Miss Tobias, "which proves men are involved."

She slowly and with great emphasis, related the experience of constable Marrow. Or Officer X as she called him. The air was electric. Even the curtains seemed to be listening. The Mother Superior's eyes were popping out. "So she revealed her identity to him?"

"Not exactly. He saw the name on her habit. Which of course had been discarded."

The incredulous figure put a finger to her lips. "So we have one bottom bouncing on the lawn and another on the sofa." She knew the furniture in Sister Martina's office from previous visits. And considered it would have been too narrow for that. Obviously not. She tried to picture the scene but stopped immediately. It was too harrowing.

It was the turn of Henrietta to feel a flash of sympathy. It must have been a great shock to her listener. True, she'd had an inkling from the original letter. But to hear it spelled out with such feeling, had brought everything vividly home. The missionary had tried to keep calm. But the enormity of it all had nearly overpowered her. Having dispensed with the facts, she added the rumours. That the men of Hatchett were being paid in kind. How many? She shrugged her shoulders. How many of them were there in the village?

The Mother Superior shivered. It was one outrage after another. She thought of the money sent to pay the bills. Now no doubt, tucked away in some high interest account. It was clear fraud. The Church was being ripped off. Yet she had to admire Sister Martina's nerve. She herself, had told her the motto to follow. 'God helps those who help themselves.' Suddenly it had become 'God help those the Mother Superior catches helping themselves.' She counted to ten. It was her way of bringing herself under control. She normally managed it after seven. But this time she had to use the full number. Plus two more.

There was one word on her lips. The one neither she nor Henrietta had dared to say aloud. Brothel. The Reverend Mother was running a brothel. There could be no other explanation. And there was no discretion.

Miss Tobias had proved that. Sex was available outside and in broad daylight. She stifled an involuntary exclamation as the full implication of it hit her. In a convent! On sacred ground! Never mind God. What if the Pope got to hear about this? She squared her shoulders. Well he wouldn't. The Church was good at hushing up scandals. This one would go no further than her. But she would have to act quickly. The convent would be closed down and its inhabitants dispersed to others. Sister Martina for example, could be sent to Outer Mongolia. There must be one there somewhere. Or Thailand or Chile. A destination far, far away. She hesitated. Yet was that the best solution? It might be spreading the sickness. Brothels could pop up everywhere. She closed her eyes. It was a tricky problem. What did her visitor think? Henrietta said the Church had to make its own mind up. But she was determined to see whoever was cavorting on the lawn prosecuted for obscene behaviour. He had to be made an example of. Her companion reluctantly agreed.

She could only hope the location would not be mentioned in court. Meanwhile she had come to her own decision. She would banish the ring leaders and install a new Reverend Mother. She might even spend a few months in charge herself. A biblical cleaning of the stables. That was what was needed. And who better to do it than a woman of her standing? She looked almost fondly at the missionary. It was said different faiths should work more closely together. What an example they were going to set! Combating sin in all its forms. The flesh was weak. And none more so than in Hatchett. In fact there, it was encouraged to be weak. The residents must be saved from themselves. Yet shamefully they did not want to be. It was the way of all humans. No wonder the world never improved. But this would be one small corner of it where God's light would shine through the heathen clouds. And under these at that very moment, another alliance of faith was being formed.

The vicar and Sister Martina were closeted together in her study. Two earnest figures planning their salvation. The meeting of the conspirators had broken up with that goal still way out of reach. The best it could come up with was a plan to delay, rather that stop, the Mother Superior's visit. It involved a long detour through a maze of country lanes to tire her out. But constable Tompkins had flatly refused to stand in the road to organise the change of direction. Having already been run over by a bike, he did not want to tempt fate again.

Ronnie had come to put an idea to the Reverend Mother which he thought might work. It would mean the protestant cavalry coming to the aid of the catholic fort. Although Ada Smith and Dora Ford could hardly be described as dashing rescuers. More like foot slogging infantry. But a valuable weapon all the same.

They both liked amateur theatricals and had taken part in the village play at Christmas. Ada had been a parrot and Dora a cockatoo in Dr Dolittle. Despite their fierce competition to be the first to receive wine at communion, they were inseparable. The vicar knew that if one was to take part, the other would have to be invited too. But that was an asset. One could help stiffen the nerve of the other. For what he proposed was not for the faint hearted. But neither of them would ever fit that description. The important thing was they would get the chance to dress up again. As nuns. They would pose as the transgressors. And there being two of them would be a bonus. Only one guilty party was expected. Sister Martina would be in the act of expelling the pair when the Mother Superior arrived. It would show how thorough the investigation had been.

Adding them to the convent's roll would have to be backdated. But that would not be a problem. And once clear of the place, they could revert to their normal selves.

Sister Martina turned the idea over in her mind. It sounded pretty far fetched. But desperate situations demanded desperate measures. And after all, the alternative didn't bear thinking about. Yes, they would try it.

Well, hopefully, replied the man of God. He hadn't asked them yet. The big plus was they were both widows. So did not have husbands who might have been using the convent's services. They would have no axe to grind. The visitor rose to his feet. He would go in search of them immediately. There was not a second to lose.

He found the pair together. Ada had popped into her friend's house for a chat. They lived two doors apart and the path between them was well trodden. They looked at the vicar with surprise. He was not known for dropping in on his flock for a cup of tea. They were more likely to meet him in the pub. But the expression on his face told them this was no chance meeting. They offered him a chair but he declined. He felt he would have more authority by towering over them. He was going to need all his powers of persuasion.

Not knowing how to start, he cleared his throat several times. So much so, that a concerned Dora offered him a drink of water. He took a sip fervently wishing it was something stronger. Putting down his glass, he coughed a final time.

"You have heard the rumours swirling around Hatchett," he began.

This was perfectly true. They had consistently helped to fuel them.

"Well," he continued gravely, "matters are coming

to a head." He then explained in detail the threat to the convent. And as he warmed up his listeners' jaws dropped. Suddenly the vengeful Mother Superior filled the room.

"But," asked Ada, "what do you want us to do?"

"Yes," chimed in Dora, "what do you want us to do?"

It was the question Ronnie had dreaded. But it had to be answered. That was why he was here. It took him back to the day of his first sermon. This time there were only two pairs of eyes fixed upon him. But they were unwavering. The butterflies in his stomach had never been friskier.

He plunged in. "We want you to pose as the culprits."

This was greeted with blank stares.

"You know, dress up as nuns and be expelled. Sister Martina would banish you just as the Mother Superior arrived. Then she could see for herself that the matter had been dealt with." He ran a finger round the inside of his dog collar. "It would all be over in a few minutes. Nothing to it really. It could hardly be simpler for actresses like you. You were wonderful in the village play."

Ada was the first to find her voice. She sounded as if she couldn't believe her ears. "You want us to come to the rescue of a catholic knocking shop?"

"I don't think we need to bring religion into it. There are protestant customers."

"And to act as tarts," added Dora in incredulous tones. "I've never heard anything like it. And from a man of the cloth too."

"It would be a Christian act."

"Christian?" exclaimed Ada. "I haven't read all the bible. But I know God is hot on fornication. And from what I hear, there was a lot of it going on. If you ask

114

me, the convent deserves to be closed."

Dora agreed. "I've nothing against catholics but she's right. Its day of judgement has arrived."

The vicar found himself going weak at the knees and finally sat down. "So you won't do it?"

"Certainly not," they cried in unison.

"I've always respected you reverend," said Ada. "But I think you've got a real nerve asking us."

"Yes, a real nerve," added Dora. "And don't think we'll change our minds."

Ada nodded. "So don't start pleading."

There was nothing else for it. Their visitor played his last card. "There's a hundred pounds cash in it for each of you."

There was a double intake of breath. Neither woman spoke, but he sensed they were wavering. He threw in the clincher. "And twenty five pounds worth of Marks and Spencer vouchers."

Dora broke their long silence. "And we get to keep the habits? Mine would go well in my dog's basket."

"Of course, of course," said Ronnie, mopping a perspiring brow with a large red handkerchief. He felt overwhelmed with relief. But at the same time appalled. He had preached endlessly against greed and the evils of mammon. And yet two of his most long standing parishioners had caved in to it without the slightest fight. But it was just as well they had. He must be grateful for small mercies. Or in this case, quite a large one.

He hurried to explain the plan before they changed their minds. It was a simple operation. Nothing could possibly go wrong. Arriving early on the day, each would be given a room. Because ostensibly, they were regular members of the Order. When the Mother Superior's car entered the drive they would be summoned to Sister Martina's office. Then as she entered the room, they would be departing. Downcast with shame, their hoods would cover their faces. They could not be recognised. Once outside the walls, they would be free to be themselves again. And at the Nag's Head, James would be waiting with two large port and lemons. Not that they would be needed for recovering, he added hastily. Just for a toast to celebrate another fine piece of acting.

"How long will we be in the convent?" asked Ada.

"No time at all, four or five hours maybe. It has excellent facilities. You'll get a decent lunch. They make a splendid soup. It's the easiest money you'll ever pick up," he added warmly. "You can laze on your beds or walk in the grounds. Then just pop into the office for a moment. And hey presto, it's all over."

Dora realised what had been worrying her. "Talking of money, when do we get it?"

"Fifty before and fifty after."

Her voice took on an edge. "Why not all before. Don't you trust us?"

"Of course I do. I'm assisting you psychologically. If I gave it all to you now, and you spent it before you went, you wouldn't feel you'd earned it. That second half helps concentrate the mind. It's following the Lord's guidance. Do good on earth and you'll get your reward later in heaven."

"I'm not sure we'll get rewarded for this," replied Dora darkly.

"You are helping one of God's houses."

"It hasn't been acting like one recently."

"It is not for us to judge, but to do," he responded, remembering dimly an old testament proverb. At least he thought it was.

He left promising to drive them to the convent when the time came. It was only a short distance, but he didn't want any last minute backsliding. They, for their part, held his crisp notes up to the light. The watermarks were reassuringly visible.

Chapter 24

A dark cloud was hovering over the convent. A sense of impending doom. The hour of reckoning was nigh. And it was having an effect on the nuns. The cheerful atmosphere had vanished. The tension was increasing almost hour by hour. What was needed, decided the Reverend Mother, was a day out. A change of scenery. Anything to lift spirits. So she hired Fred Dunnet and his old coach. No, he could not be paid in advance. But Sister Adela could sit right behind him. They would take a packed lunch. The picnic's theme would be the Sermon On The Mount. They would find a hill somewhere and at the top she would deliver a little homily. To buck them up. It would have a much better effect in the fresh air. Her audiences tended to nod off in the stuffy interior of the convent.

Fred was an experienced operator. If they felt sick, he said, as inexperienced travellers, they should tell him immediately. He was good at emergency stops. But nobody did. It was a bright and breezy morning and that quickly became the mood of the party. Sister Martina was right. They all needed to get out.

After driving for an hour, they decided to look for somewhere to halt. Several of them were feeling peckish but they were not allowed to eat on the coach. Fred did not want crumbs on the seats. There had seemed to be hills everywhere before. Now there were none. The countryside was increasingly flat. Yet the Reverend Mother was determined to find one. You couldn't have the sermon on flat ground. It just wouldn't be the same. And anyway, some nuns were taller than her. She wanted to look down on them. She had almost given up hope, when she saw a small rise behind a farm house. That would do if they could get permission. A fat woman in an apron opened the door. Sister Martina explained their plight. Her listener called over her shoulder to a hunched figure at the kitchen table. "They want to borrow our hill out the back for a picnic."

"I don't want holidaymakers running amok."

"They're not tourists, Colin. They're nuns. Something to do with the Sermon On The Mount."

"Is that the one about the loaves and the fishes?"

"I don't know anything about that. They've got packed lunches."

"All right. As long as they shut the gates and don't leave litter."

The party trooped to the top and spread themselves out. Sister Martina took possession of the summit. "If anybody has to answer the call of nature, please avoid the skyline."

Sister Rebecca put her hand up.

"What is it?"

"I've forgotten my boiled egg."

"I'm sure somebody will give you half theirs. We all know it's better to give than receive."

There was hasty swallowing.

The speaker sighed. "I don't know what's happening with this convent."

Once lunch was over, she asked for their attention. "I will give you exact instructions on the day, but we must prepare for the battle ahead. The three Rs will be called for. We have to be righteous, resourceful and resolute. And also in times of crisis we must enlist those three Cs. We need to be careful, crafty and cunning. We must fight fire with fire."

The onlookers shifted uneasily. This was meant to be a day out. They didn't want the frighteners put on them. The Reverend Mother sensed their mood. They were right. The idea was to give everybody a break. But she couldn't help herself. They could not afford to

119

be caught with their habits down. Otherwise they would be picnicking every day in the wilderness. She organised a game of tag. Soon there were shrieks of laughter as the nuns picked up their hems and raced about. The couple below watched through their lounge window.

"Must be some sort of religious rite," said the wife.

"As long as they don't stray into other fields," replied her husband. "If they do, I'll send the sheepdog to round them up."

Beryl watched the scurrying black and white figures. "I've been thinking. Why don't we ask them to pray for our girl. They are here and they don't look too busy."

"I don't know. I could ask. But it seems a bit silly."

"How can it be silly? A prayer never hurts. They are good at it. And there are a lot of them. It would be more powerful than any we could do."

Colin got up. He knew his wife would just go on and on. "All right, I'll do it."

He made his way slowly to the top of the hill. The Reverend Mother stepped forward to greet him. Where her girls causing a disturbance? He shook his head firmly. No, no. He had a favour to ask. Certainly, what was it? He scratched his neck pensively. Could they say a prayer for his Maureen? His listener's face clouded. How important was it? It was their day off. And they didn't often have one.

Colin gave a discreet sigh. "It's the wife who wants it really. It will only be a quick job. Nobody will have to kneel."

"Can I do it on my own?"

"Beryl thinks it will make more impact if you're all at it."

"Very well, where is she?"

"In the barn."

Sister Martina frowned. "In the barn?"

"Yes, she's a cow."

Her voice carried a note of surprise. "You want us to say a prayer for a sick cow?"

"Yes, animals are as important as humans. To us farmers anyway. And I expect to God."

The Reverend Mother tossed the idea in her mind. Why not? They'd been so busy praying for themselves they'd neglected everybody else. The Lord would appreciate their effort. It might even help their cause. She clapped her hands. "Sisters we will take a short break. We have a simple task to do. Follow me."

They trooped down the field into a dusty outhouse. Maureen lay listlessly in a pen of straw. Her eyes were dull and reproachful. She barely lifted her head as they gathered round. Sister Martina had no book with her. So she was restricted to prayers she knew by memory. Running through them in her mind, she was gratified to realise how many there were. Picking one that would do equally well for man or beast, she led the chorus. It was all over in a few minutes. There was no visible effect on the patient. As yet. But her owners were delighted. When the visitors left, Colin presented them with six bottles of his own apple juice. Running about and praying are thirsty work so they were passed around on the coach.

They had returned to it breathless and happy. They surprised Fred pouring over the Page Three girl in the Sun. He tried to hide it in his embarrassment. No, no, they cried. They'd like to look at her after him. To keep up the good mood, Sister Martina called for a sing song.

A couple of lively psalms and a rousing hymn encouraged the driver to follow with In Dublin's Fair City. Fortunately, most of this was drowned out by the engine. Yet several nuns tried to join in. Even if they didn't know the words. This lack of decorum startled the Reverend Mother. It was most unusual. Then she noticed that many faces had become increasingly red. And that a lot of giggling was going on. A suspicion dawned on her. She took the nearest bottle and sniffed it. Cider. So much for Colin's innocent apple juice. The whole party were getting drunk before her very eyes. She moved swiftly to collect the rest. Yet she was too late. Nearly all were empty. And it took a tug of war with Sister Olga to retrieve the only one that was still a third full.

The Reverend Mother watched her charges disembark. It would be fair to say that most fell, rather than walked, off. She tried to remain positive. If the object of their outing had been to let the nuns let their hair down, it had been a great success.

The following morning she received a phone call from the delighted farmer. Maureen had really perked up. She didn't tell him the cow would be feeling a lot better than those who had prayed for her.

Chapter 25

Hatchett too cast aside its looming troubles for one day. The Britain in Bloom judging was taking place. Near neighbours, Puckford, had beaten it in the past two years. To concede a hat trick was unthinkable. There were rumours the rival village used plastic sunflowers in its impressive displays on the church tower. None of the inspectors had ever been brave enough to climb up and sniff them. To rub salt into the wound, the winning committee had come over the last time to celebrate at the Old Venice. As they were mainly male, Ant had withdrawn the services of Linda and Tracey and looked after them himself. He was pleased to note the more subdued atmosphere but was grateful for the business.

The gardens had been neck and neck. It was the hanging baskets which had made the difference. So this time Hatchett had put in a stupendous effort. The result was six of the finest imaginable. A perfect blend of greenery and colour. Yet the other half dozen were not quite so excellent despite the constant attention lavished upon them. All that could be done was hope for the best. Or so it seemed. An idea was forming in the back of the colonel's mind. But he couldn't work out what it was.

Hatchett had two main streets with the baskets divided between them. The six finest were to be seen first. Early impressions were all important. It was while the judges were looking at these, that the penny dropped in the military brain. The route took the party down past the duck pond and the church and up the other side. It would be twenty minutes before they reached the second lot. Enough time for them to be switched. With a short cut, it was just a little distance. But a row of houses lay in between. The colonel picked the one directly opposite. The baskets were swiftly lowered. He, the vicar, and the newsagent, picked up two each. They were almost bent double under their weight. One by one, they lifted themselves and their precious burdens over the back fence. They crossed the lawn to the side gate. It was locked. The colonel tapped on the lounge window.

Inside, Terry Hines was watching racing from Kempton Park. His wife was doing a crossword.

"Is that a bird?" he said. Most of his week's pension was riding on Lady Diana well placed on the inside rail. Vicky went to the window and opened it. "No, it's the colonel."

"Can you open the gate?" pleaded the intruder. "We are in a desperate hurry."

"It's always locked to keep the cats out. I don't know where the key is."

"Then we'll have to come through the lounge."

She turned her head. "Terry, there are three of them. They want to climb in here with a lot of hanging baskets."

Her husband was transfixed to the screen. The runners were entering the home straight. "We don't need any hanging baskets. Tell them to try next door."

"They aren't selling. They just want to come through."

"They'll have to wait until the race finishes."

"They can't wait. They're in a rush."

"If they're in a rush, they'll spill earth everywhere."

"That's true. And I've done my hoovering for the week."

"We won't spill anything," declared the colonel. "And we really have no time to waste. Please take these."

He handed his two to Vicky who put them on the floor. He climbed in and the others followed.

"Damn and blast," came a cry from the set. Lady Diana had finished fifth.

"Don't swear Terry," ordered his wife. "We've got visitors." She looked at the new arrivals. "Have you got time for a cup of tea?"

"No, it's very kind but we really haven't," replied the vicar who already laden, was heading for the door. He was used to spending hours perched on parishioners sofas. Such a hurried departure was a novel experience.

Out in the street, the three got to work. There was no sign of the judges although the sound of distant voices was drifting towards them. Ronnie found himself praying desperately for time. It was the first occasion he could recall that he had done so without putting his hands together. They were far too busy. As were those of his companions. Down came one lot of baskets. And up went the other. Everybody's arms were aching. But fortunately all the hooks were low enough to be reached on tip toe. Ladders were not needed. The first heads of the inspection party came bobbing round the corner as the trio beat a hasty retreat

Terry was hoping for better luck in the 3.30. The front doorbell rang. "What is it now?" he demanded.

"It's them again," replied Vicky. "And they've still got those baskets."

"No, they're different ones," replied the colonel"

She stood aside to let them in. "Have you got time for a cup of tea now?"

"I'm afraid we're still in a tearing hurry. We have to hang these up before the judges get back."

They tramped past the punter on the sofa and clambered out into the garden. Arthur who brought up the rear, called back "if we win the award, it'll all be down to you."

"That's nice," said Vicky. "Very nice."

The judges returned to their cars without a second

125

glance at the ones they'd already seen. Just as the colonel had thought they would. He knew all about psychological warfare. He wasn't just good for crawling about in the bushes. In due course, Vicky got her bouquet. "How kind of you to bring it through the door," she said.

In the evening there was a barbecue on the green. The feeling was the inspection had gone excellently. Everybody was cheerful. And it was just as well Henrietta was not there. She always felt uncomfortable whenever anything was cooked on a spit. It reminded her of her grandfather. She imagined him being turned this way and that. And then being cut up into chunks.

James had erected a beer tent to save people trekking to the pub. It did a roaring trade. As the sun sank over the trees, a large number of pints went down with it. As did quite a lot of whisky and not more than a few gin and tonics. Yet the inhabitants of Hatchett could hold their drink. There was only one accident. Norman tripped over a tent rope after half a glass of bitter. But he had his helmet on as usual. So no damage was done.

Chapter 26

The plane touched down smoothly at Heathrow. Bambini made his way through the customs' green channel. He had nothing to declare but a murderous thirst for revenge. This time there was nobody to greet him. He was glad. He was in no mood for small talk. First he would go and see Pedro in Finchley. Then, with that comforting bulge under his arm pit, he would head for Hatchett. He allowed himself a rare smile. It was a perfect day. Henrietta's last few hours would be filled with sunshine. He did not begrudge her that. He liked to despatch his victims in good weather. It was the least he could do for them. A frown flickered across his face. Although hers might take a little longer. He did not know exactly where she was. But anyway, he said to himself brightening, the forecast was for clear skies to continue. And he was sure it would not take him long to track her down.

Yet later that afternoon, his own dark clouds were gathering. They swirled round inside his head as he drove his hire car out of London. Pedro had changed his address. He was now residing in Pentonville Prison. And would be doing so for the next five years due to an unfortunate slip up in his gun smuggling. His tearful wife had given his visitor the last remaining weapon. An old colt forty five. She had spent a most uncomfortable two hours sitting on it in her armchair while police searched the house. Her husband had had no chance to bury anything in the garden. This was just as well, for the police had dug it up. That had been the only bright spot. She was busy planting potatoes, aubergines and onions in the freshly turned earth when Bambini arrived.

As a hit man, he had been banking on a smooth little

automatic with a silencer. Handling the colt, he felt more like his American boyhood hero, Jessie James, rather than Don Coreloni. But a gun was a gun he reasoned, trying to be positive. And he had his cord and his knife with its razor sharp blade to back it up. Which would he use? He still had to make a decision.

It was almost dark when he arrived at his cousin's restaurant. He could see a scattering of diners through the window. Not bad, he thought, for a midweek. He went round the back. It was an embarrassing return after the rocks fiasco and he did not want too many onlookers. He hoped nobody would mention the coffin. The English were said to be tactful. This would be a good test. But honour would be restored with the death of the missionary.

Ant put down the plates he was carrying with an exclamation of delight. He feigned surprise. But his smile was a little too fixed and his slap on the back a little too hearty. Bambini's finely tuned antenna twitched. "Antonio, you knew I was coming?"

"Yes."

"Your aunt Maria?"

"Yes."

"That woman, she cannot keep her mouth shut. I will kill her." Seeing his cousin' worried face, he added quickly, "metaphorically speaking."

After consuming platefuls of heaped spaghetti served by a somewhat suspicious Rosa, they settled down for a talk.

The restaurateur knew he was wasting his time, but he had to try to stop what would be a cold blooded murder. He pointed out the situation had become more complicated. Miss Tobias had hired a bodyguard. He had been seen in the village. A small but muscular man with a hard face and moustache. Bambini took the news in his stride. So there would be a shootout. He had been

128

in many. You had to crouch low to minimise yourself as a target.

No, no, protested his cousin. This was Hatchett, not Palermo. There must be no stray bullets. The hit man nodded agreeably. The wine he'd drunk with his meal gave him a pleasurable glow. It would probably come down to the knife. Which was why he had chosen his tie so carefully. It was of two different shades of blue. One dark, one light. When he wiped the blade on it, Henrietta's blood would provide a perfect contrast. It would make it go even better with his suit. Or his grey pullover if it was too hot for his jacket.

Ant misjudged his softening mood and tried once again. "There is no need for the woman to die," he pleaded. "How they say in English? She has already spilt the beans."

Bambini's half smile vanished. "It has nothing to do with beans. It is now a vendetta. And you know Antonio, how that works." Rising, he poked his cousin in the stomach with a stubby finger. "Beans, beans, beans. How many beans she spill eh? Who cares. It is blood, blood, blood. How much blood you spill. That's what counts."

Ant was taken aback by the ferocity of the words. He felt like that about football but not killing. A wave of panic swept over him. What could he do? He would warn constable Tompkins but he would need reinforcements. And the police would not act on such wild hearsay. The first priority must be to alert the intended victim. But where was she?

At that moment, the back door clicked. Rosa had gone to find out. She had listened to the conversation with practiced ease as she scurried about the kitchen. And now she was moving even faster. Fear gripped her heart. She could not believe what was happening. Her husband was a good man. But he would sit in his chair and throw up his hands in horror. She was the one who had to act. And quickly. She hurried through the darkness towards the cottage. She felt a surge of relief. There was a light on. At least somebody must be at home. Not bothering to close the gate, she pounded on the door. A window opened somewhere above her. "Who's there?" said an uncertain voice.

"It's me, Rosa," came the urgent reply. "You must let me in."

"Are you alone?" asked the cleaner.

"Yes, but I won't be for long."

Mavis, Henrietta and Donald Chambers had arrived back from the meeting with the Mother Superior a short time before. They, like everybody else, had been in conference. The missionary had concentrated all her thoughts and energy in presenting her report safely. Now that was done, she suddenly worried about her own. Whoever had put her in a coffin temporarily, may now be intent on doing it permanently. This question was quickly answered. A breathless Rosa. emphasised that 'may' had become 'definitely would.' She refrained from adding 'as soon as possible.' She could see Miss Tobias was agitated enough as it was.

Yet she hardly lightened the atmosphere by asking the detective if he was armed. He said he was not. It would be a case of grabbing the nearest chair leg. Mavis gave an involuntary look around the room. She was fond of her furniture. If it came to a fracas, she hoped it would not happen here. Although if it did, the stool in the corner looked the most useful weapon. She gave an ironic laugh. If Rosa was right, what good was that and her mop against a gun, a knife and a strangling cord? It was obvious Henrietta would have to flee. Both she and Mr Chambers forcibly pointed this out. Ant's wife nodded her head vigorously in agreement. But the fugitive stood firm. God had set her a task. It was not yet done. She would not tire or falter under the heavy load.

"Discretion is the better part of valour," the detective advised with conviction. "It is wiser to live to fight another day".

"The fight is now," replied the missionary adamantly. "We must stay the course."

"But it is nearly over," said the cleaner. "The wrong doings of Hatchett have been exposed. And the Mother Superior is arriving to punish the convent."

The missionary's breath came more sharply. "But we have not identified the bottom."

"I don't believe God will worry too much about that," said Mavis.

"No," agreed the detective. "I think he would consider it immaterial."

"Immaterial?" retorted Henrietta. "It certainly is not. It's owner was obscenely committing adultery. And his sins must be laid before the Lord. And of course the courts."

"We're not absolutely certain it was adultery," ventured the cleaner.

"It has to be," said Henrietta confidently. "Virtually every man in the village is married. You said so yourself."

"This conversation is getting us nowhere," warned the detective. "We have to decide what to do. If Miss Tobias refuses to leave, we must find her somewhere to hide. The cottage will be too dangerous."

"Nowhere is safe," added Rosa who had been an avid listener. "You do not understand an Italian vendetta. Bambini will not rest until his mission is completed. Then he will love Henrietta. He will send huge bunches of flowers to her funeral. And with it a card."

The detective became interested. "What would it

say?"

Rosa shrugged her ample shoulders. "'Sleep well my little bird. It was nothing personal.' Something like that."

"But it seems to be personal," pointed out Mavis.

"It doesn't appear like that when the victim is dead. The emotion goes."

"Well, what blooms would he chose?"

"Lilies are most popular. But whatever is in season."

"And the wreaths? Are they big?"

Rosa's eyes gleamed. "Yes. Sometimes it takes two men to carry one. But they lay it so tenderly."

Henrietta shifted uncomfortably in her seat. "I'm not dead yet," she almost shouted.

The three came to their senses with apologetic looks.

"We were being hypothetical," Mr Chambers said reassuringly. "There will be no murder in Hatchett. Not if you lie low anyway."

"I cannot do that," replied the missionary. "I promised to meet the Mother Superior at the convent."

Walking home, the restaurateur's wife had a wild idea. It was late and Bambini would be asleep. He liked to get in the full eight hours before a kill. She told her worried husband where she'd been. He nodded in approval but was strongly against her plan. It was to steal his cousin's weapons. In the end he reluctantly agreed it was the only way to disarm him. She would tiptoe carefully into his room. It would only take a minute. In the morning they would show surprise at their loss. And even help search for them. But by then they would be buried in the woods. It was the safest place. Bambini would immediately rummage in the dustbins.

Armed with a small torch, the intruder softly opened the door and made her way towards the bed. Her wavering beam picked out the sleeping figure. The cord was wrapped firmly round his wrist like a bracelet. The knife in its sheath, was strapped to the inside of his leg. The gun looped round his neck by string, nestled under his armpit. He may have been in Ant's house. But anywhere outside Naples was enemy territory. There was no way she could remove any of them without waking him up.

Rosa returned white faced and empty handed. Her husband gave her a consoling hug. They had done their best. The missionary had at least been warned. It was funny, he mused. First the villagers had set out to get rid of her. Now they would have to try to save her. He thought of his cousin's ice cold eyes. If indeed they could.

Chapter 27

Ada and Dora were waiting at their respective gates for the vicar. They had only been given twenty minutes warning to be ready. But that was plenty of time. Their stay would be so short, little was needed. Only the clothes they wore and a case to carry these home after being swapped for habits. Both had only had toast for breakfast. If the food at the convent was as good as it was said to be, they intended to make the most of it. They felt a certain tenseness in their stomachs but that was to be expected. It was always the same with a new show.

Ronnie looked them over. They had obeyed his instructions to wear no make up. It gave them a certain freshness even if they did look a few years older. But still young enough for their parts. He for one, liked mature women. Had they any last minute problems? No, they had not. Did they understand their roles perfectly? Yes, they did. Were there any questions? Yes, when would they get their other fifty pounds? As soon as they had completed the job. When they returned from celebrating at the pub, they would find the envelopes pushed through their letter boxes.

The vicar drove slowly to let his passengers compose themselves. But the short journey was soon over. The pair got out gingerly and surveyed their new surroundings. The convent had always been a building in the distance. Now it loomed over them, slightly menacing. Suddenly a hundred pounds did not seem enough. They steadied their nerves. As the vicar had said, it would be a piece of cake. And speaking of cake, it was nearly lunchtime. Their driver escorted them to the door and rang the bell. Then he discreetly retired, muttering a short prayer. It carried a lot more feeling than many he had uttered in church.

He drove home telling himself he had done all he could. It might be a far fetched and even risky plan. But it was the only one that had any chance of working. He glanced at his watch. The Mother Superior was due in three hours. Just about the right length of time. Long enough for Ada and Dora to assimilate themselves. And short enough to stop them from getting bored and beginning to wonder what they had let themselves in for. At least he would not be in the firing line. He thought of the first world war padre who told soldiers departing for France. 'God go with you. And I will go with you as far as the station.' He felt a slight stab of guilt but it did not last long. It was not like that with him. He would be on hand. Just a few hundred yards away if anything went wrong. But what could he do? Precious little. If the cat got among the pigeons, Sister Martina would have to sort it out. The sun emerged from behind a cloud to light up the sky. He felt a surge of optimism. Of course everything would be all right. His two actresses would revel in it. No doubt in their youth they had been close to being tarts. They looked the sort. He hastily banished such ungrateful thoughts. That was not being fair. They had become regular worshippers and loyal members of his congregation. And now they would be his heroines.

He stopped at the pub to order their drinks. They'd deserve every drop if they pulled it off. And if they didn't? He shuddered. The sun had gone behind a cloud again. Suddenly the future looked gloomy. James agreed they would be large ones and on the house. The girls, as he called them, would certainly be feeling thirsty. He admired Ronnie's plan for its simplicity. To be truthful, he could foresee a few tricky moments when the Mother Superior arrived. But only a few. He had watched Ada and Dora in the village play and was impressed by their performances. Maybe a little too theatrical at times but that could be what was needed. It would be high drama in Sister Martina's office. The landlord admitted he would like to be a fly on the wall. The vicar took a gulp of his much needed gin and demurred. The tension would be great. Much too great. James took the glass and added another shot from the optic. "I shouldn't be doing this. You should be praying not drinking."

"They go together in times of crisis," said his friend, pouring more tonic. "I gave thanks to God for their safe delivery at the convent. Now I feel another one coming on."

"What's this one going to be about?"

"Giving them courage to take on their task."

"Can I join in? It would give it more power."

"Certainly. What a good idea. Repeat after me." The vicar bowed his head and put his hands together. "Dear Lord, please guide Ada Smith and Doreen Ford with a firm hand on their day of destiny. Give them the strength to take their acting to new heights. And to -."

"What's this?" said the doctor entering the bar. "I thought these were licensed premises, not a church."

"We're trying to make sure the plan works," explained the landlord.

The newcomer ordered a whisky and gave Ronnie a commiserating pat on the back. "No offence old boy, but praying's too hit and miss. You should have come to see me first. I could have given them something from my little black box. You know, to cheer them up, steady their nerves. That sort of thing."

"We all know your tonics George," he replied. "We don't want them confronting the Mother Superior as high as kites. Their adrenalin will be flowing fast enough as it is."

The doctor appeared lost in thought. "Where will it

end?" he asked staring out of the window. "Will she be fooled? Will the convent be able to resume normal service? Or will she unmask the owner of that bottom? Or bottoms. Will the village be full of tear stained wives and husbands pleading for forgiveness?" He peered round at his silent companions. "You do well to look grave. And what about Miss Tobias? Will we need another coffin? This time for real?"

"Listen George," interrupted James. "Doctors are meant to have a bedside manner. To cheer patients up. Lift their morale. You make us feel as if we are on death row."

"We all could be," came the serious reply. "I like to tell the truth. Once I gave a man six months to live when I knew he only had three. He booked a cruise and died going up the gang plank. His wife was unable to get a refund. I will not make the same mistake again."

The vicar eyed the clock on the wall. To him it resembled a ticking time bomb. "You will not have to wait long for some of your answers. The Mother Superior is due in less than two hours."

"In that case, we'd better have another drink," said the landlord. The three of them drained their glasses and put them none too steadily on the bar.

Chapter 28

Ada and Dora each had a second bowl of soup. It could have done with a little more salt. Otherwise they had no complaints. Everybody seemed friendly in a silent fashion. There were smiles and sympathetic glances. But no words. Sister Martina felt this was the best way. It would enable the visitors to concentrate fully on their task. She wanted to call them saviours. But that at this stage, would be tempting fate. The big hurdle had yet to be cleared.

The pair had donned their habits straight away to get used to wearing them. They agreed that they did make you feel pious although they were a bit itchy round the neck. The two soon became fidgety lying on their beds and went for a stroll round the grounds. They inspected the lawn. So that was where the dreadful deed had taken place. It was quite close to the wall. The missionary would have had a good view all right. They imagined her eyes popping out.

They returned to find the Reverend Mother asking for them. There was still an hour to go. This was for a final briefing. She had greeted the pair with a nod when they had arrived. Now her handshake with each was long and firm. And she poured a generous amount of brandy into their cups of coffee waiting on the table. Also residing there was a bowl piled high with peppermints. In case the worst came to the worst, and they ended up within sniffing distance of the Mother Superior.

Sister Martina spoke with studied calm as she watched the visitors for any sign of wavering. But there was none. The curtain was about to go up and they were ready and waiting in the wings. First, they had to remember their names. One had to be Sister Adela because her identity was known. Or so the Reverend Mother presumed. Ada plumped for that, leaving Dora to chose Flora. It was estimated the Mother Superior would take three minutes to reach the office from her car. The front door would be already open to prevent her bad temper from becoming even more ferocious. As Sister Martina greeted her, the pair would scurry out heads bowed in shame. Followed by the Reverend Mother's blackest looks. The avenging presence would then be told of their appalling fall from grace. How Sister Adela had given in to her desires and Sister Flora had followed out of curiosity. The fault of gossiping after lights out. They were being banished into the wilderness. With the investigation over, there was no point in the Mother Superior staying. But she must have tea after such a long journey before returning home.

"What about the identity of the bottom?" asked Ada. "Surely it will have to be in my confession."

"You don't know it."

The would-be nun looked incredulous. "Don't know it?"

"It's owner came up behind you and put his hands over your eyes. Things went from there."

"Went where?"

"Where they can go in these situations."

What about afterwards?"

"They stayed shut."

"Was I in ecstasy?"

"No, praying for forgiveness."

"The Mother Superior won't believe a word of it."

"But she can't cross examine you because you won't be here. That's the beauty of it. She'll have to accept what's in the confession. Identity unknown."

Sister Martina handled a sheath of papers on her desk. "These are both your statements. They have been carefully prepared by the vicar and myself. There is no need to bother you with them. You will be gone before they are read. Suffice to say you had several moments of weakness. Which, men being men, took full advantage of." She looked at her watch. "Zero hour is approaching. You must go and compose yourselves. And I must do the same." She gave them a weary smile. "Good luck to us all."

Chapter 29

The colonel toyed with his steak and kidney pudding. It was his favourite lunch, but he had a lot on his mind. "Damn silly idea of Ronnie's to send those two old windbags to the convent," he said prodding a potato.

"That's a harsh description isn't it?" replied his wife. "I see you leering over Dora's figure every Sunday when she goes up for communion."

"All right," he admitted. "They're still young enough for the parts they're playing. But the roles."

"What do you mean?"

"Nuns. Do they look like nuns? They're more like fish wives. They'd be better off as bingo callers than saying prayers."

"But they won't be saying any will they? They will just slip past the Mother Superior and be gone. That's the plan."

Her husband sighed with exasperation. "The first thing the military teaches you is that no operation goes smoothly. You have to have back up. Plan B. The vicar has nothing. I offered to help. But no, he and Sister Martina had it all under control."

"I suppose they thought too many cooks would spoil the broth."

"Cooks? They're more like students opening a tin of baked beans. The outcome is going to be disastrous."

Alison wore an amused smile. "You mean the Mother Superior will discover the owner of the bottom and then we'll all know." The colonel turned a shade paler. "By we," she went on, "I mean the wives. It's all the women talk about now. Whose husband is it? Or rather husbands."

"It's all rumours," said the rather restless figure opposite her. "That's another thing the military teaches you. Never listen to rumours."

"Tell that to Mrs Gardner. She's opened a book on the result." The speaker leaned forward. "And you are well up the field."

The colonel went from white to red.

"Not a front runner, it is true," his wife continued. "But at ten to one, certainly in the frame."

He laughed a trifle nervously. "This is total nonsense."

She appeared not to hear him. "There are two at six to one and three at eight to one. Do you want to know who they are?"

He held up his hands in horror. "I don't believe a word of it."

"Most women are betting first on their own loved ones. Not that they're sure. It's insurance. Just to have some consolation winnings if the worst happens."

He could not stop himself. "And you?"

"I've risked a fiver. I'm not too suspicious, but I wouldn't put it past you. You've paid enough visits with that firewood."

The colonel struggled to take in this latest development. "That missionary has got a lot to answer for."

Alison nodded sombrely. "That's what we've got to discuss next. I hear she is in great danger."

"Yes. Bambini is coming back. That is, if he is not already here."

"And he really would kill her?"

"Certainly. The mafia do not forgive being crossed."

"What? In an English village?"

"Anywhere in the world. They have a long reach."

"Well we must stop it."

"No, I am looking forward to the funeral."

"This is no time to be funny. We will have to go to the police."

"It would be a waste of time. We have no proof of anything. And the scenario is far too preposterous for them to believe in it."

"Then we must act ourselves."

"What do you suggest?"

"You have plenty of connections. What about your friends in the SAS?"

"We're all retired now."

"Once a soldier, always a soldier, that's what you told me. The sight of a few uniforms could frighten off Bambini."

"You can't have a dad's army hanging around the village. They'd drink the Nag's Head dry."

"Well, it would give you a rest from doing it. All that's needed is a couple of sentries outside her cottage until he gets the message."

"It's not Buckingham Palace. And most of them would be as stiff as boards after standing guard for half an hour."

Alison sighed. "It was only an idea. We have to do something."

"The best thing Miss Tobias can do is hide. She won't leave the village. It's not in her nature. If she goes to ground he won't find her."

"She'll need help for that. And not many villagers would step forward."

"That's true," he agreed. "It is a most worrying situation."

Chapter 30

Mrs Gardner was the widow of Sam the bookmaker. She liked to keep the wagers coming in his memory. It was all under the counter, so to speak. But she was trusted and always met her obligations. She kept the odds reasonably short. Especially after once having to sell an armchair to pay a punter. Brenda was a cheerful woman of ample proportions and a quick mathematical brain. She was adept at sizing up what her clients would bet on. She immediately saw the potential of the bouncing bottom. It made a refreshing difference from which garden would produce the first snowdrop or crocus. But what odds to put against the suspects? She was a resourceful gossiper. As she had to be. And had heard all the rumours. And she knew the leading candidates. Rogues all of them. Likeable rogues, but still rogues.

Those deemed to be front runners felt a secret pride mixed with public indignation. Several made half hearted attempts to have themselves placed further down the field. Brenda met all demands with a benign smile. It was the bookmaker that made the odds. Not the horses. Money poured in. It was her most successful venture. A substantial number of his congregation backed the vicar. Was that loyalty or inside information? The pub's regulars likewise went for the landlord. Did they know their man? There was also a respectable following for the doctor among his patients. Constable Tompkins and the newsagent also had their supporters along with the colonel whose denials in a clipped military tone, impressed no one.

Mrs Gardner had to concede it was certainly a tricky subject. She was convinced all the leading contenders had made that special visit to the convent. Whether in the fresh air or not. As a widow, she'd had the eye from most of them at one time or another. The colonel had bounced her on his knee at the Christmas party with military precision. And the doctor always seemed to brush past her when there was plenty of room to manoeuvre. As for the vicar. Well, talk about 'not being led into temptation.' He needed to heed his own words.

She was counting the latest takings when there was a knock on the door. It was little Rufus Potter from the gift shop who had been included to make up the numbers.

"Come in. What is it?"

"I'm not happy."

"Oh, for being on the list?"

"No, for the long odds. I want to be higher up."

"Really?"

"Everybody's laughing at me. I can put it about just as well as the rest of them."

"I'm sure your wife's pleased you're down the field."

"No, Rita isn't. She thinks it makes her husband look a wimp."

"Ok. I'll bring you up to twenty to one. Is that all right?"

"Yes. And I'll have a fiver on myself. But don't say who put the bet on."

Brenda shook her head as he left. "Men."

Chapter 31

It was rare for the colonel to summon up such a hearty welcome. "Good morning Jenkins. Have I told you recently how much I appreciate your work? As a small token I hope you will take these." He produced four cans of Guinness still cold from the fridge. "It's the least I can do. We should all try to help each other." He blew out his cheeks pensively. "While we are on the subject, I wonder if you could do me a small favour?"

His handyman gave what could be described as a slight wince.

"It really is only tiny," went on the speaker. "Hardly anything at all."

"It's not to do with the convent is it?"

His employer reacted with surprise. "Why yes, it is. It's those bundles of firewood I've been delivering. I was wondering if you could say you did it."

"Did what?"

"Took them up to the nuns instead of me."

"Sorry colonel, I've heard the rumours too."

"You have?"

"Yes, and I've seen the book."

"What book?"

"Mrs Gardner's. Your odds are attractive. I've been thinking of having a tenner on you myself."

His listener stiffened. "This is no time for jokes."

"I'm not joking. It could be a good investment."

"Listen Jenkins, this is no laughing matter. There's no point in beating about the bush. I'm a pillar of local society. The whole thing of course is nonsense, but I can't afford to be in the firing line. I've got my reputation to think of. The honour of the regiment and all that."

Jenkins's voice hardened. "And I can, is that it?

146

Because I do odd jobs I'm expendable. I'd like to oblige, but I'm an innocent man and won't be put in the frame."

"I'm innocent too."

"Of course you are."

"That's what so awful. Being under suspicion for something you haven't done."

"I'll tell you what. I'll say I drove you there and waited in the vehicle. I know it's perjury. But I don't mind swearing you were never more than five minutes. You couldn't do much in that time could you? Not with your dodgy knee."

The colonel rubbed his chin thoughtfully. "I suppose it could work. You won't change your mind about delivering them yourself?"

"No."

"Well it's better than nothing and I'm grateful. With luck it will never come down to it. The trouble is you never know what turn an investigation will take."

The handyman sounded intrigued. "If it's not you colonel, who do you think it was having a go on the lawn?"

His listener just managed to control his irritation. "You don't have to be uncouth. It's not a subject I'm prepared to discuss. It's a very tricky situation all round."

Chapter 32

The brandy had given the two actresses a warm glow. But had worn off all too soon. Their mouths were dry and their hands clammy. Ada began humming to keep her spirits up. But had to stop because it annoyed Dora. Likewise her friend's foot tapping was quickly forbidden. Both agreed they needed to listen for the car. Even though they would be summoned immediately. There were several false alarms. More than one visitor was due that day. Finally the door flew open and they were on their way. Their hearts beat in time with their feet as they hurried down the corridor. Sister Martina was standing by the window. They joined her. They watched the Mother Superior climb out of the vehicle. She wore a dark cloak wrapped round her austere figure. Her eyes roved in their direction. They could not be seen, but instinctively ducked. She strode towards the front door, a young assistant trotting at her heels. There was no time to lose. Sister Martina began to berate her would be saviours in dramatic fashion. It was a bizarre scene for neither had done anything wrong. But an oppressive atmosphere was essential to greet the Mother Superior's entrance. It was the first act of a life and death play. The second and last, would be their abject departure in front of the bemused guest. And for this they had to appear suitably shaken. Sister Martina's angry words ricocheted round the room. They seemed to bounce off the walls and collide directly over their heads. It was an impressive sight which greeted the convent's interrogator.

Yet there was no sign of fury on her brow or flash of anger in her eyes. She was graced with an air of immoveable serenity. She hated modern travel. She wished she'd been born a thousand years ago. Then she could go by mule like a proper pilgrim. But it had been a perfect journey down. Drivers had given way to her at every crossroad and roundabout.And those forced to queue behind her stately progress had not given one toot. Even when she slowed to fifteen miles an hour to admire a rainbow. No, they had waited to pass at the correct places. It made her realise the essential goodness of mankind. It was a parable showing the value of patience. And she would heed it. She had set out to bring fire and brimstone. Now she would offer forgiveness and understanding. It was human to err. There must be a lecture, yes. Transgressors must be shown the error of their ways. But then allowed once again to find the path of righteousness. That is what the Lord would want.

She stepped in front of the two figures scurrying towards the door and held up her hand. Their heads were bent low but she sensed their anguish. This was because neither was able to squeeze past. Sister Martina intervened. "These are the culprits of our investigation," she declared. "There is not one, but two. They have admitted their guilt and shown no remorse. They are being instantly dismissed."

"But why are we showing them no mercy?" exclaimed the Mother Superior.

Caught off guard by this unexpected retort, their executioner floundered. "But they don't want mercy. They have realised the Order is not for them. They are happy to leave."

"Nonsense. They are troubled children. We will succour and care for them." She looked at the pair who were feeling faint and had their eyes fixed on the floor. "I have news to lift your hearts. You will return to stay with me. Together through prayer and meditation, we will go back to the Lord."

Her listeners were stunned. By now they had

149

expected to be on the way to the pub. Their port and lemons seemed a long way off and they needed them desperately.

The Mother Superior beckoned her assistant. "Sister Claire, take these poor sinners back to their rooms and help them prepare for their journey. I am afraid it's only a small car so you will have to sit on one of their laps."

Sister Martina watched the trio disappear, wishing she could go with them. It was not the time to be left alone with the Mother Superior. Her forgiveness was disconcerting and she was sure it would not last. And what about the fate of Ada and Dora? That did not bear thinking about. She cleared her throat nervously. It felt parched after all her shouting. "A cup of tea to celebrate?"

Her visitor raised her eyebrows. "Celebrate what?"

"The cleansing of the stables. The ending of the investigation."

"One cannot celebrate the downfall of two of our flock."

"But they are no longer of our flock. They have shown themselves to be unworthy. They must be banished."

The Mother Superior frowned. "I will be the judge of that. But tell me, did they make full confessions?"

"Yes, I have them here."

"And so we know the owner of the bottom?"

"Not quite."

"What do you mean not quite? It is either yes or no."

"No."

"And why not?"

"The sister involved had her eyes closed. She was praying for forgiveness."

"A likely story. But there were other occasions?"

"Yes."

"And we know the men?"

"No."

"Why not?"

"Customer confidentiality"

The Mother Superior seemed to have difficulty taking this in. "Customer confidentiality? They have no right to that. They have been fornicating on sacred ground. They must be punished for their sins. Then," she added, remembering her parable, "we will forgive them. I will talk to your two fallen sisters. They will tell me the perpetrators of these dreadful deeds. God demands the truth and I will be speaking in his name."

There was a knock on the door and Sister Claire entered. Tears streamed down her face and her voice quavered. "They've gone." The two onlookers stared at her. She began sobbing. "They went over the back wall."

The Mother Superior pointed to a chair. "Sit down child and explain yourself."

"When we got to their room they just packed their bags and marched out. They crossed the lawn and then one got on the shoulders of the other to climb up. On the top, she reached down to pull the rear one up. But she was too heavy and pulled her back on top of her. They landed in a heap. They picked themselves up and went to a shed where they got out a ladder. They put it against the wall and both climbed up. Then they pulled up the ladder and used it climb down the other side."

The Mother Superior's face was a picture of consternation. "What were you doing while all this was happening?"

"I just stood there."

"You did not try to stop them?"

"No."

" Why not?"

"They said something to me."

"What was it?"

Sister Claire blushed profusely. "A word that can never pass my lips."

"Then write it down child."

Given a pen and paper, she hesitated a moment before inscribing two words. One of four letters, the other of three. The second word was 'off.' Her two companions stared at them before Sister Martina hurriedly scrunched up the sheet and threw it into her waste paper basket.

The Mother Superior put a hand to her head. "I trust this sort of language is not current at the convent."

"Of course not. I told you they were not suitable for our Order."

"I can see that now. And as they have departed, I agree the investigation is at an end."

Sister Martina tried to keep the rising hope out of her voice. "And the bottom?"

"That too, I am afraid. I am most reluctant to let the matter drop. But now we have no option."

The figure opposite felt a wave of elation sweep through her. She had an insane desire to leap up and start dancing. It was over. The convent was in the clear. It took a huge effort to stop herself from clapping. Unfortunately it was not a southern Baptist church. It was all down to the vicar's crafty plan. Who'd have thought he had it in him? And those two actresses. They might have done a runner but they never chickened out. They played their part. Not a bad contribution from the protestants to be fair. If she had another lottery tip off, she would make sure St Andrews shared the numbers. It might bring better luck. And in fact after this great escape, she would buy several lucky dips for Ronnie to hand out to his congregation. She remembered her visitor with a start. "Now we can have a pot of tea before you go. Sister Agnes has made a nice Madeira cake."

The Mother Superior surveyed the table. "We will need another cup. There are only two." Seeing her hostess's puzzled look she added "Miss Tobias is popping in. I arranged to meet her here. I felt she should be on hand as it was her complaint. Of course it's all academic now. But our gathering can herald a new dawn."

Sister Martina suddenly went cold inside. That woman had a cheek showing her face. Admittedly she could no longer cause trouble. The investigation was dead, but it was the last place where she would be welcomed. She wondered if Bambini would come to her aid. She'd heard he had returned. There was plenty of cover on the way up from the village. A single well aimed shot from the bushes and it would all be over. She felt a stab of guilt. Reverend mothers shouldn't think like this but it was the missionary's own fault. Busy bodies deserved everything they got. And in her case, the sooner the better.

The Mother Superior by contrast, was all warmth and sympathy over what was now a wasted journey. But Miss Tobias took in neither approach. She wore a startled expression and was breathing heavily." I have just seen the most extraordinary thing," she declared. "I couldn't believe my eyes." She sank into a chair. "As I came up the path, two of our parishioners came flying past dressed as nuns. They almost knocked me down."

"You must have imagined things," said Sister Martina.

"Oh no, I recognised them immediately. They were Ada Smith and Dora Ford."

"How could you with their hoods up?"

"No, they were bobbing behind them. They were moving so fast."

"I have to say it's a suspect identification."

"Certainly not. I see them every week in church."

Sister Martina sensed the Mother Superior's eyes on her. And they were very penetrating. The cold feeling had disappeared. Now she felt unbearably hot. She was dying to open the window. And jump out of it. She could feel several questions hanging in the air. And they were all aimed at her.

Chapter 33

The vicar was waiting outside the Nag's Head when the landlord opened up. "I want to witness the triumphal arrival," he said. "They should be here at any minute."

"Don't worry," replied James. "I'll have their drinks ready. If you ask me, nobody will have deserved them more." He poured two beers and taking his, went and stood by the window. "Why," he exclaimed, "here they come now."

Ronnie moved towards him but he held up his hand. "Wait. Judging by their expressions, I think you'd be safer in the other bar."

His companion frowned. "What do you mean?"

They don't look triumphal to me. More like bent on revenge."

"Do you think something's gone wrong?"

"I don't run a pub for nothing. I can tell a customer's mood as soon as they walk in. And theirs doesn't look too good. Not good at all." The vicar stood undecided. "Hurry up," urged his friend. "I don't want any furniture smashed."

He retreated as the pair entered. The landlord was behind the bar already pouring their drinks. This was no time to delay. He put their glasses before them. They each pulled up a stool. There was silence. But it was electric. First one took a large gulp. Then the other. Their eyes were closed. James pondered what to do. Their faces it had to be said, were grim. Very grim. But how to lighten the mood? He drew on his vast experience. "Are you having a nice day?"

This went over their heads. They seemed to be reliving a traumatic experience. It was Ada who spoke first. Her fists were clenched and she had difficulty getting her words out. "Where's the vicar?"

The landlord took a tankard off a hook and began polishing it nervously. "You mean good old Ronnie?"

"Yes," replied Dora in a voice that cut through the air liked a knife. "Good old Ronnie. The man of God who sent two innocent members of his flock to the slaughter."

"Steady on. You're still here."

"If being kidnapped by the Catholic Church isn't slaughter, I don't know what is."

The landlord put down his tea towel. "You were kidnapped?"

"We were indeed. Because we were in the front line. And where was the Reverend Perks? Safely in the rear. Skulking in his bunker behind our skirts."

This was too much for the furtive figure hovering by the connecting door. "That's unfair," he cried bursting in.

"Is it?" replied Dora. "You're worse than the money lenders in the temple. You bribed two vulnerable women with cash to do your bidding. Instead of giving us strength, you took advantage of our weaknesses. You should be excommunicated."

"Yes," added Ada. "And then shot."

The object of these desires felt he had to sit down. Motioning for their glasses to be refilled, he ordered a large gin. Then he appealed for calm. Recriminations were all very well. But what had happened? He and James had no idea. Pacified by another double each, mainly of port, the pair told in lurid detail what had occurred at the convent.

"But if you escaped without being interrogated," said the vicar at the end. "The plan is still intact. There may have been the odd moment of anxiety but it was a success after all."

Ada shook her head. "I'm afraid not. When we were fleeing we passed the missionary and she had a good

156

look at us. She was obviously on her way to meet the Mother Superior. The cat will now be out of the bag." She drained her glass a second time. "We'd better drink to Sister Martina. She's going to need all our best wishes. Never mind our prayers."

She certainly will, thought Ronnie, making a mental note to give her a wide berth for the next few days. But the immediate task was to mollify the two actresses who continued to glare balefully at him. But that was easier said than done. He looked at the flustered figures. "Danger suits you," he said conjuring up his most admiring tone. "It has brought a becoming colour to your cheeks."

"And a sparkling gleam to your eyes," added the landlord helpfully.

"Don't sweet talk us," replied Ada angrily. "That's nothing to the one that'll be in the Mother Superior's when she hears what the missionary's got to say."

"And it will serve both of you right," said Dora. "I don't know why we got involved. We must need our heads read."

The two men privately agreed. Although this was not the time to say so. But the widows had been the last card to play. There were none left in Hatchett's hand. There could be no more dealing from the bottom of the pack. There wasn't one. Nor was there an ace up anybody's sleeve. The village could only await its fate.

Chapter 34

Sister Claire had been dismissed. Sister Martina sat facing the Mother Superior and Henrietta. She longed for a lever to pull. The trap door would open beneath their feet and they would vanish like the young novice. Hopefully never to be seen again.

The interrogator had removed her assistant for a good reason. Her ears were far too young to hear what she had to say. She produced her sternest expression to give her words extra impact. Not that they needed it. Her feelings of goodwill and forgiveness were disappearing at an astonishing speed.

"So the whole thing was a set up," she declared. "You brought those two women in to pretend to be the culprits. I have to say it was a harebrained scheme. And it would not have fooled Miss Tobias and myself for an instant." She picked up the two confessions. "Among the mistakes you made is one vital one. I have looked at the names you chose, Sister Adela and Sister Flora. Neither matches that of the transgressor." She shot Sister Martina a patronising look. "You did not think we had it, yes?"

The recipient of this glance was confused. As far as she was concerned, it was the real Sister Adela. And she had been desperately wishing she had hidden her somewhere.

Henrietta handed the Mother Superior a piece of paper with a flourish. The Mother Superior already knew what was on it. But she made a show of studying it intently. It reminded Sister Martina of an Oscar ceremony but the next minute she could not believe her ears.

"Sister Bridget." declared the speaker with chilling conviction. "Sister Bridget is the one who has strayed so badly from the path of the Lord."

Pure relief mingled with disbelief, gripped the embattled figure. She had to force back a strong urge to giggle. Sister Bridget was known as Little Mouse. If there was one of her Order who would never look at a man, it was her. But how had this ludicrous mistake been made? She thought hard. Of course, it was her habit. Sister Adela would have borrowed it to seduce the policeman. And the name would have been inside. She always liked to wear one a size too small when conducting business. It showed off her assets better.

Sister Martina was a picture of tranquillity as she faced her accusers. Would they like to see Sister Bridget now? Yes they would. The sooner she confessed, the quicker her redemption could begin.

The Reverend Mother rose to her feet. "I will go and get her."

Chapter 35

Bambini awoke with the early morning sun on his face. Carefully removing his weapons, he padded to the door. The thread across it had been broken. Who had entered? Henrietta's body guard? No, he was still alive. It was more likely to be Rosa. He would have to watch that woman. Even among friends he was in the midst of enemies. He repeated the phrase. It had a certain ring to it. He ate two slices of pungent cheese for breakfast. He liked his breath to smell strongly when confronting a victim. Especially if he was using the cord. He would have preferred onions. But it was too early in the day for them. Returning to his room, he put his pistol and ammunition into a plastic bag. Then he headed for the restaurant's large dustbin and fished out six empty cans. Cramming these on top, he made his way into the nearby wood. There, he set them up along a low branch. He had to get the feel of the colt. He liked to play act. It gave his practice shooting greater intensity. His favourite scenario was Al Capone and the St Valentine's Day massacre. But he didn't have a machine gun. So it would have to be the gunfight at the OK Corral. He couldn't be Wyatt Earp. The sheriff was too tall. He would be Doc Holiday. The pistol was heavy in his hand and jumped as he pulled the trigger. But he still got four of the six at the first attempt. Not bad from a half crouch at twenty paces.

The muffled reports attracted the attention of Norman who was taking his customary stroll around the village. Edging through the foliage, he came upon the Italian in the act of reloading. Bambini looked up to see a helmeted figure half hidden in the undergrowth. He froze. Helmets meant soldiers or bodyguards. It could only be the missionary's enforcer. A feeling of near panic gripped him. He had been caught with an empty weapon. Always keep one bullet in the chamber, his grandmother had told him. Why did he never bother to listen to her? He forced a smile. "I have no quarrel with you my friend."

Norman failed to take this in. "Are you shooting rabbits?"

Ant's cousin uttered a coarse laugh. A good joke. Victims were just like rabbits. The stranger knew the score and had a sense of humour. But be careful, he warned himself. Don't be lulled into a false sense of security. He had been under surveillance. He shuddered. This man had tracked him here away from prying eyes. He went cold inside. Was this to be the showdown?"

Norman did not have much conversation. He relied on the last big event in his life. "Have you seen the coffin?"

The hit man stiffened. The rabbits had been a joke. This was not funny. What was he trying to say? He wished he could slip in another cartridge but they were nestling in the bottom of his bag. He felt naked. He had left his knife and cord in his room. His standards were slipping badly. And here he was facing a cold blooded professional. It was a time for steady nerves. He peered at Norman who was searching for a follow up line. He had met his sort before. The strong and silent type. A bit like himself. But something was troubling him. Suddenly he realised what it was. His counterpart had been described as small, but muscular with a moustache. This one was taller and skinnier. Unless he was a master of disguise, there were two lined up against him. He was outnumbered and in a foreign country. He steadied himself. He'd taken on bigger odds. It had been four to one in Parma. But luckily, he'd been standing behind his opponents. Yet there was no way he could get to the rear of this one. He was far too crafty. That was a nasty bramble patch in between. He had picked his spot cleverly. A master of field craft. That's why he'd followed him noiselessly.

Norman found his voice again. "It's made of lovely pine."

Bambini flinched. It was bad luck to keep talking about coffins. It was all right putting people in them but not to make a song and dance about it. He put up his hands in mock horror. "They are not for us my friend."

Norman felt a surge of gratitude. The reassurance was wonderful. So he would definitely live to be a hundred. He thrust his hand into his pocket. The world stood still for Bambini but all that came out was a white paper bag. "Have a sweet," said its owner emerging into the glade. The Italian dug in a finger and pulled out a toffee. His companion did not seem so forbidding after all. Then he realised who he was. The half witted boy. He had often seen him wandering about on his previous visit. He was angry with himself. Who was the most half witted? What was it his grandmother had said? The best killers have no imagination. He had let her down once more. A harmless figure in a helmet had become an ogre. Well, it would not happen again. No, it was a timely lesson. He was glad his mafia compatriots were not watching. He could hear their sniggers. Louder than any gurgle when he pulled the cord tight. The next gurgles to be heard would be Henrietta's. And speaking of Henrietta.... He put his arm round Norman's shoulders as they walked back through the trees. "You deliver the papers, yes?" His companion nodded. "So is Miss Tobias at her cottage?"

"She was there, but she's going away."

His listener's brow darkened. "How do you know?"

"She said she didn't have time to read hers this morning. She was going to -." He stopped, trying to remember. Bambini gripped his arm. "Where? Where?"

Norman's face cleared. "To the convent. She is going to visit the convent this afternoon."

The hit man smiled broadly with relief at the news. He had at last marked his prey.

"Another sweet?"

The Italian pushed the bag away. "No thank you my friend. I am too excited to eat. I have a much bigger treat in store."

Chapter 36

It took Ada and Doris time to recover from their escapade. All actresses like their shows talked about. But not this one. Not these two. No, they were not converting to Catholicism they kept saying. The whole village had the same joke but it was not funny. Ada had taken up smoking again after three years and Dora was rolling her own in increasing numbers.

That first Sunday their pews were left empty. After the service, a concerned Ronnie went to see them. Sitting in Dora's lounge, they refused to talk to him. He had to enlist Mrs Robinson, a neighbour, as a go between. She had a rasping voice which was not far off a loud hailer. He feared the whole street would hear. They had sent him to Coventry. And the church. He should be ashamed of himself for tempting them with riches. Yes, they had spent the hundred pounds, thank you. Ada had a winter coat and Dora a warm rug for the spare bedroom. But they wished they hadn't. They felt guilty. They would have given it back only it was too late now. And the same for the tokens. They'd gone on some nice blue underwear. To match the bruises they got climbing over the wall. They were too private to show him.

Ronnie's effort to speak quietly and persuasively was being ruined by his words being repeated at almost a fog horn level. He stressed it was unfair to bring God into it. By not going to church, they were sending Him to Coventry as well. The pair shook their heads in determined fashion. No, they weren't. They'd said their prayers right here in this room. He wouldn't just be concentrating on the service. He listened to everybody. Wherever they were. That's what the reverend had said himself. And, in their own way, Ada added, they had taken of Christ's blood. She pointed to a bottle of sherry on the sideboard which was three quarter's full.

"That doesn't count," declared the vicar. "It's only Christ's blood when it's been blessed. That's why you have to go to church. It's no good swigging it at home."

"We're not swigging it," Dora replied hotly, forgetting Mrs Robinson was there. "We sip it."

Their visitor felt like saying he couldn't remember either ever sipping anything, but felt the moment was not opportune. He desperately wanted to bring them back into the fold. His congregation was small enough as it was. He had an idea. "That nice family from the farm filled your pews in the front. They did enjoy sitting there. They asked afterwards if these were now free." He paused. "I said I'd find out."

The two errant worshippers exchanged glances.

"I'm afraid it's a squatters' rights system isn't it? " Ronnie went on. "If you return in the future you can always sit further back. There's usually plenty of room there."

The speaker could almost hear their brains agonising.

Ada spoke first and directly to the vicar. Mrs Robinson, increasingly redundant, had gone home to lunch. "We have yet to decide our future movements. But I think you'll agree, those are our pews."

"You have a claim, yes. But unfortunately St Andrews is not a restaurant. I can't reserve them. Especially if they're not going to be used."

His listeners had another look at each other. They seemed to read each other's mind.

"This is a serious matter which requires discussion," said Dora."Would you kindly wait in the kitchen."

The reverend took himself off sensing a gleam of hope. He knew that no vouchers would tip the scales this time. In less than five minutes he was called back.

"You are right," said Ada. "We feel it unfair to punish the church for the misdeeds of it's vicar." Ronnie opened his mouth but she held up her hand. "We too have strayed by taking your pieces of silver. So we are putting you on probation. And ourselves. Blessed are those who can point the finger who have not also sinned."

"Yes," added Dora. "We believe people in glass houses shouldn't throw stones."

Ronnie felt his spirits rise. "So I will see you both next Sunday?"

Ada gave him a still slightly disapproving look. "It would appear so."

"And I am no longer being sent to Coventry?"

"Well, we seem to be talking to you."

"Will it last?"

"As long as you behave yourself," Dora said archly.

That's an awful cheek, thought the vicar. But what could he do? He had to keep his flock together. Even if they were two irritating old ewes. No, he mustn't think like that. They had tried to help and suffered a nasty fright for their pains. And they were certainly an asset to his services the way they belted out the hymns. Their eyes followed him to the door. He wondered in turn what they were thinking. Probably something you would never dare say in church. But at least he'd brought them round.

Chapter 37

Sister Bridget sat demurely with her hands clasped on her lap. She had left the Welsh valleys as a young girl to enter the Order and had never regretted it. She had been summoned to Sister Martina's office twice before. Once to be complimented on her neat sewing and once for the fervour of her singing. Scurrying at the Reverend Mother's heels, she had wondered what the third would be. The length of her prayers? Or her work on the marrow patch?

Her mouth had dropped open at the sight of the Mother Superior. But she had quickly composed herself. The important visitor was less settled. One might almost say, fidgety. There was no sign of her forgiveness returning any time soon. What was meant to be a thorough and impressive investigation, had so far turned out to be a farce. Well, it would be ended now. And swiftly. There would be no more softly, softly approach. She would not exactly get Sister Bridget by the throat. Everything must be conducted calmly and methodically but there would be no fussing around. She would go directly to the point. She thrust a pen and paper in front of the somewhat startled figure. "Write down the names of every man who has fondled you," she demanded. 'Fondled' was her only concession to delicacy. It was the closest she could think of to the word which must never be used.

The young girl looked to Sister Martina for help. Her ears could not believe what they were hearing. The Reverend Mother was only too pleased to elaborate. "Well, think very hard. The Mother Superior and Miss Tobias are anxious for the answer. All those males you entertained. Who are they?"

Her listener was becoming more confused than ever.

If she had any emotional weakness, it was a slight hankering for Sister Beatrice. Sister Martina was well aware of this. She had seen them holding hands during a carol service. But there was a game to be played. And she had to play it for her own survival. It was unfair that Sister Bridget had to be sacrificed, but when the injustice of this accusation was revealed, there was a good chance the Mother Superior would throw in the towel. With Sister Adela remaining undetected, there would be no one else to point the finger at.

The girl in front of them partly resembled a traffic light. She turned a greenish hue and then bright red. Sobs began to wrack her body. Her world was being turned upside down. How could Sister Martina say such lies? "You know these things aren't true," she cried in anguish.

"I do, but I have to reiterate them for our visitors. They say they have proof."

The victim could take no more. Rising to her feet, she ran blindly from the room. The Reverend Mother watched her go. She made no move to stop her. Her companions appeared shocked. She acted quickly to strengthen her advantage. "Sister Bridget is clearly innocent but the doctor is due soon for our check ups. She will have one extra test. This will prove conclusively that she is fully intact where it counts."

A rather dazed Mother Superior turned to Henrietta. "This does seem to be so."

The response was grim and determined. "We must not give up. I saw what I saw. If I was imagining it, Sister Marina would not have tried to dupe us. There is no smoke without fire."

Her fellow interrogator appeared to waver, but then slapped her knee in a show of vigorous agreement "You are right. I shall stay the night. And tomorrow we will interview the entire order. There will be no absentees. If anybody is hiding in the sick bay, I will see them there."

The Reverend Mother fought to hide her disappointment. She said nothing but managed a sickly smile.

It was time for Henrietta to go home. She looked out of the window. Dusk was falling. The gathering shadows made her feel uneasy. What if Bambini knew she was there? She thought hard. No, it was most unlikely but what had Mr Chambers said? If there was the slightest whiff of danger, never take a chance. That seemed good advice. Especially in her current situation. So after being shown out of the front entrance, she turned sharply left instead of taking the main path. Walking round the back of the building, she climbed a stile into the meadow that ran alongside it. She cautiously followed its hedgerow to the edge of the village. The twinkling lights in the windows made her brave again and the final yards along the road held no fears.

She was greeted at the door by a worried looking Mavis. "I thought that Italian had got you. I was expecting you hours ago." She ushered her in. "Our detective had to go. He's forgotten to ask a neighbour to feed his cat. But he'll return in the morning."

The missionary gratefully sipped the cup of coffee thrust into her hand. Then perched on the sofa, she told the cleaner everything. Her friend sat goggle eyed. What a to-do. So if it wasn't Sister Bridget, who was it? That, replied Miss Tobias, was the big question but it would certainly be answered tomorrow. The Mother Superior was not one to be crossed. And once she confronted each nun in turn, the guilty one would wilt. She stopped for a moment, picturing the scene. The list of fornicators would come tumbling from a pair of frightened lips. And Sister Martina would sink to her knees, begging forgiveness. Her hands would be clasped tightly together. Her head bowed in shame. It was almost a biblical scene and a very satisfying one. And where would she be? She would be there to congratulate the Mother Superior on a triumphant finish. Or Sybil, as she called her in their more intimate moments. It proved the worth of the old adage. If at first you don't succeed, try, try and try again. She fought back a smirk. One must be magnanimous as far as possible. No one was perfect. But certainly some were more perfect than others. And she could not help but put herself in that category.

Left alone, the Mother Superior felt the need of fresh air. But not in the grounds. Not where the nuns could watch her through the window. She liked to skip a little when she walked. It got the blood flowing. But it was hardly dignified for one of her station. And she needed to think without distraction. Sister Martina had been running rings round them. Or trying to. But no longer. Once she got the order assembled before her they would be like terrified rabbits. She often practised her piercing gaze in front of the mirror. When on form, she was surprised it did not crack. And she would be on form tomorrow. There was not the slightest doubt about that. She had taken prayers that evening to make her presence felt. Just to give everybody something to think about. And of course it had worked. The responses were loud and clear and if anything, a trifle over eager.

She let herself out of the front door and made her way to the path. It was pleasantly warm with a gentle breeze. It rustled the leaves enough to deaden her footfall. And that of the crouching figure approaching from behind her. She got a whiff of stale cheese and everything went black. Bambini's fingers tightened relentlessly. Then he suddenly loosened the cord. Her opening gasp had been a strange one. Nobody knew a gurgle like he did. But he'd heard Henrietta talk, and it was not her. He laid the limp figure on the grass. And the neck. He'd inspected the missionary's when putting her in the coffin in readiness for such a day. This had a prominent Adam's apple. Hers did not. The killer instinct had got the better of him in the darkness. He should have made a closer inspection. His victim was the same height as Miss Tobias and with a similar figure. He'd have noticed straight away if he'd attacked from the front. But you always strangled from behind that was the problem. There must be quite a few cases of mistaken identity. He wiped his brow. And this had nearly been another. The Mother Superior was breathing but still unconscious. A livid bruise was already forming around her throat. The contrite hit man cupped some water in his hands from a puddle and threw it on her face. Her eyes flickered open and she stared up at him. "Spiacente", he said and quickly vanished into the gloom. The hapless figure lay as if in a dream. Had she fainted? Who was that apparition? Her neck was incredibly painful.

She could not bear to touch it. She groggily got to her feet and stumbled towards the convent. She was plagued with dizzy spells and found it increasingly difficult to breathe. Back in her room, she examined herself in a looking glass. An angry red weal shone vividly above her crumpled collar. It was turning purple before her eyes. Then she remembered the sensation as she blacked out. The flurry of an arm and something pressing on her windpipe. A desperate struggle for air. And that aura of cheese. Was it gorgonzola? Or could it have been mozzarella? She wasn't sure. Maybe it was ricotta. But that was immaterial. What mattered was somebody had tried to kill her. There could be no other explanation. And why had they stopped? It looked like a professional attack. So the assassin's conscience would not be involved. But there must have been a change of heart because he'd apologised. "Spiacente," he had said. And she knew what it meant. It was Italian for 'sorry.' She'd heard it several times when her toe was trodden on as she entered St Peter's Square to see to the Pope. But why hire a foreign hit man? She shook her head. It was all a mystery. It was clear only that somebody wanted her dead. And as far as she could work out, there was only one suspect. Sister Martina. She had the motive and the nerve. She would give her that. In the morning she would confront her. But now she urgently needed to get some sleep. Taking her bedside chair, she stuck it under the door handle. God would protect her ,but sometimes he might require a little help. She snuggled down under the covers. Her neck was throbbing. It had been a close call. She wondered again what had saved her. It could only have been divine providence.

She awoke finding it too painful to talk. She couldn't lower her chin because of the swelling. That meant looking straight ahead. She would have to bend her knees to see anybody shorter. She sighed with frustration. There could be no immediate show down with Sister Martina. And no interviewing. Not for a while.

The Reverend Mother could not have been more sympathetic. She called for pen and paper and after reading a scribbled version of what had happened, swiftly rang for the doctor. When he arrived, she conferred with him gravely. The result was a most careful examination of the patient's condition. Followed by a strict instruction that she must not speak for three days. Sister Martina had wanted five, but George said that was stretching it a bit. Three should be enough to work out how to shield Sister Adela from the storm that was certain to come.

Chapter 38

Donald Chambers had intended to be bright and early at the cottage. He was early, but not feeling very bright. After feeding his cat, he'd had a few whiskies. Either three or four. Or maybe five or six. He couldn't remember. But he'd needed them. Who wouldn't in his position? He'd turned from being a detective into a bodyguard. And being nearly fifty with a paunch, he was hardly suited to the role. How on earth had he got into such a pickle? And all because of a bare bottom. At least his wasn't the guilty one. If Miss Tobias had kept cycling instead of being nosey, the whole saga would never have begun. But it had, and he was in the middle of it. For all his failings he was not a quitter. And having been hired by the missionary he would stick by her. But the future filled him with foreboding. Most of the village was dead set against her. And leading the pack was that murderous Italian. He hoped he wouldn't have to come to grips with him. It was too late now for a karate course.

He paused at the front door. His fist raised indecisively to knock. What was the signal again? They had devised a code to bar any intruder. It was either three short, two long, one short. Or three long, two short, one long. Or a combination of both. He should have written it down. His head throbbed as he concentrated. He was rescued from his dilemma by Mavis. She had been hovering by the lounge window and let in the dishevelled figure. She was greeted by a cloud of alcoholic fumes but said nothing. It was not surprising he needed a drink. She continued to restrict herself to one sherry a night. But she had started to use a larger glass. Henrietta was preparing to go to the convent to hear the interviews. The detective despite his hangover, offered to accompany her. She gracefully demurred. She would be safe at that time of the morning. Rosa had revealed that Bambini always had a good lie in. She would ring if she wanted to be escorted back. She set off at a brisk pace and met nobody on the way.

She was greeted by the normally effusive Mother Superior with a hesitant nod. She then read the note which explained why. She had hardly finished when another was thrust in front of her. It contained only nine words. 'It was Sister Martina who tried to kill me.'

The missionary shook her head. "No, it was me."

Her hearer snatched up her pen and wrote. 'Of course it wasn't you.'

"No, no. I mean it was me they were trying to kill."

Henrietta went on to explain it was a case of mistaken identity. They were of similar build and could easily have been taken for each other in the darkness. Bambini must have known she was visiting the convent and had lain in wait. She however had taken a different route home as a precaution and this had nearly caused the Mother Superior's death. The speaker's voice quavered. She would never have forgiven herself if that had happened. She looked at her mute companion. Everything would now have to wait until she could talk again. So what would she do in between?Apart that is, from trying to stay alive.

This was of grave concern to the Mother Superior. Realising her friend was too restless to be locked away, she offered a guard of her own nuns. They would rotate their duties. Two hours on, and two hours off. Henrietta had a fleeting vision of walking down the street surrounded by a phalanx of swirling habits. It was hardly a threatening sight. But even the most hardened desperado might blanch at taking on a Holy Order. Even so, she refused the kind offer. She already had her protection organised. And it was quite adequate. She was sure her escorts would have done a good job but their religious duties must come first. And the local roads were unsuitable for sandals.

The doctor called again to examine the victim. Henrietta remained to study his bedside manner. Butter would not melt in his mouth. Yet she was certain he had helped put her in her coffin. Despite his smiles, she wouldn't trust him an inch. She thought of the tonic he had given her. It was still in the cupboard and that was where it would be staying. She sensed he was in collusion with Sister Martina. She was another picture of concern poised in the doorway. The missionary's imagination took hold. If I wasn't here she thought, they'd put a pillow over Sybil and suffocate her. Then her face would go as purple as her neck. Looking at the heavy bruises, she realised the assassin had only just stopped in time. It was a stark reminder of the danger she was in. If it had been her, he would have continued to tighten the cord. No doubt with a smile on his lips. She put a hand to her own neck. It felt worryingly vulnerable. At least if garrotted rather than hung, she wouldn't dangle. It was important to appear dignified in death. She pulled herself up short. What was she thinking about? This was no time to be negative.

She looked once more at the patient. George was gently patting her hand and Sister Martina was straightening the counterpane. She had just lovingly adjusted the pillows. Henrietta had seen many hypocritical scenes but never one to match this. It was nauseating to witness. As that coarse saying went, it was enough to make anybody want to throw up. Not that the Mother Superior could at the moment because of her throat. She wondered how much the visitor was being taken in. She was a clever bird but there were a lot of crafty people in Hatchett. And none more so than the two fussing over her. But the Mother Superior had played her cards right so far. She hadn't been sidetracked by Sister Martina's games. She had said she would get to the truth swollen Adam's apple or not. The missionary felt a slight stab of guilt. If she had not made a detour, this would never have happened. But then again, she herself would be dead. So it had been a sacrifice worth making. She hoped the victim saw it like that.

The patient began sipping fruit juice through a straw while Sister Martina held the carton. The sight was almost too much for the onlooker. She was certain the effort to get round the Mother Superior would fail. But if it went on like this for two days, there might be the glimmer of a chance. And she was powerless to stop it. She had no reason to be at the convent until the interviews started. Sister Martina had twice said goodbye to her in the clearest of tones and the doctor had offered her a lift. She decided to walk. If she got into his car she might never get out again. You just didn't know who you could trust.

She arrived back at the cottage to find an anguished Rosa hopping from foot to foot. Who had Bambini murdered? She thought it must be the missionary until Mavis had explained she had been alive and well that morning. The Italian had come home last night and washed his cord. That was a sure sign there had been a killing. It was a matter of hygiene. So many necks today were not kept properly clean.

Henrietta sat down and told her story. How Bambini had stopped just in time. Rosa nodded. Yes, it made sense. He normally lit a candle for each victim and let it burn to the end. She had seen him take one from a restaurant table, light it, and immediately blow it out. That would explain the unfinished job. She put her hand to her mouth as the extent of his deed sank in. He had half strangled a most exalted figure in the Catholic Church. His own religion. He would need at least a hundred candles lit for himself to even begin to atone for his crime. And he certainly wasn't going to have the Old Venice's supply. But this nonsense would have to stop. She would get Antonio to be firm. No, that was no good. She would have to do it herself. And quickly. Miss Tobias would not be safe until he was back in Italy. If necessary she would drive him to Heathrow herself. Although it would mean a long journey. She only ever used the slow lane.

But how to protect the missionary in the meantime? She knew Bambini. Once the cord had been half pulled, it would have to complete the journey. It was like those tribal clans where a dagger once drawn, had to be used. She thanked her lucky stars that Henrietta was not alone. She had Mavis who was a resolute companion. And of course her investigator who was also her bodyguard. She looked across at the detective who was sleeping off his hangover on the sofa. Three cups of black coffee had failed to keep him awake. But it had to be said, he was within reach of a chair leg in case of a sudden attack.

Rosa promised to confront the assassin. But in the meantime, she devised a warning signal. The restaurant's flag pole could be seen from the cottage. When Bambini went out, she would hoist a red dish cloth. When he was at home, it would be a green one. The ever practical Mavis asked what happened when it was dark. The missionary must be safely locked up by then. They must on no account open the door to anybody. What if it was a friend? said the cleaner. Rosa sighed at her naivety. Bambini could be standing behind with a knife at their back. He was up to all the tricks. They would have to be constantly on their guard to outwit him.

She made for the door with a heavy heart. They were a hopeless rabble. What they needed was six months in the back streets of Naples. Then they would know how to look after themselves.

Rosa found Antonio's cousin sitting in the kitchen; a steaming plate of macaroni before him. His cord was drying on the arm of his chair. He never let it out of his sight. Especially when a job was half finished. She wasted no time. Her anger made her brave. "You must stop this campaign at once. Do you know you nearly killed a Mother Superior?"

Bambini shrugged. "She was in the wrong place at the wrong time."

"No, you were in the wrong place at the wrong time. And you're in the wrong country. Your task is finished here."

"My task is to kill that woman. So it is not finished."

"This is all going too far."

"It is a matter of honour."

"Honour? Killing a defenceless missionary?"

"It has been ordained."

"By who?"

"Me."

"Well, it's time you stopped your ordaining. We have all had enough."

Ant's cousin affected not to hear. He took a large mouthful and dabbed his lips with a napkin. Rosa's eyes glinted. The interview might be over for him but not for her. She raised her voice. He might believe he was an honourable member of the mafia, but he wasn't. He was a coward. A sad figure. A little man. She might well have been whispering. Mouthful followed mouthful without any recognition that she was there. This was familiar. Suddenly she realised he was adopting her husband's tactics. This was Antonio when she wanted to give him a lecture. Sitting like a stone.

Or in the case of this more forbidding figure, a rock. He was immoveable. She knew she had failed to make the slightest impact. All she could do, was to help protect Henrietta as best she could.

The next morning the fugitive looked out of the window. The red flag was flying. She glanced at her watch. Only nine o'clock. Bambini had forsaken his lie in. If he couldn't sleep, he must really mean business. She gave a shudder. But only a slight one. She felt safe enough at the cottage. Particularly with her companions. Mr Chambers was now installed in the spare bedroom. And feeling much more livelier than yesterday. Mavis was out cleaning, but would come back with the latest gossip. Did the village know what was going on? Henrietta suspected it did. Nothing happened in Hatchett without everybody knowing. So did they want her dead or alive? She suspected dead. Well, all those with transgressing bottoms. And she was certain there were plenty of them. But what of the one she saw? The one causing the whole furore? There could be nothing worse than going to her grave without knowing its owner. She would be turning in it constantly. Well, that wasn't going to happen. She stepped back from the window. Rule number one, don't expose yourself. She sighed. If only the mysterious culprit had followed that advice.

Chapter 39

Donald Chambers slipped an Italian dictionary into his pocket. He'd underlined several words so they could be easily found. Like 'friendship' and 'brother.' He would try the soft approach first. He'd heard Bambini could speak a little English. But it would help the atmosphere if he could meet him halfway. He'd known all along there would have to be a showdown. But it tightened the muscles in the stomach. He was beginning to appreciate how Gary Cooper felt in High Noon. Even though he was not taking on five villains. He sensed the Italian would be enough on his own.

The detective had been tempted to disappear but somehow he couldn't. He admired Henrietta for not compromising. Everybody else he knew in life did. She was like a Kamikaze pilot. She had buzzed around the village and was now crash landing on the convent. The outcome of the investigation was immaterial to him. His bottom was not in the frame. But he had been hired to help solve the mystery. And felt keeping her alive was part of the bargain.

The problem was how to confront her would-be assassin. His approach had to be circumspect. Otherwise before he could speak, he might find a knife stuck in him. It was Rosa who came to the rescue. He had confided in her while keeping it a secret from Henrietta. Bambini did not always eat in the kitchen. He liked to dine alone in the restaurant in the early evening. Without fail, he sat in a certain corner seat with his back to the wall facing the door. There was nothing sinister in this. It was just a traditional mafia precaution. She would cook him his favourite ravioli. That would put him in a good mood. She would also keep the 'closed' sign in the window to make sure the place stayed empty. The detective must walk in and sit himself down at Bambini's table. Tracey or Linda would be sent immediately to get his order. It would all be very civilised. Antonio's cousin was unlikely to depart. He found it extremely difficult to leave an unfinished plate. And being on home territory, would not feel threatened. She suggested a dish of carbonara. It was another of his favourites. And he might want to follow with his own helping. With it being awkward to talk with one's mouth full, they could weigh their words before speaking. All in all, the best solution possible. Mr Chambers could only think of one better. Confronting Bambini in a barber's shop while he was having a shave. Unfortunately there was not one in Hatchett.

The sun was beginning to sink below the horizon when he set out. It was a cool evening but he felt the perspiration on his brow. Could he talk some sense into the Italian? He doubted it, but he had to try. He had no plan of action. He would play it by ear. He had not the slightest idea of the reception he would get. All he could do was appeal to the Italian's better nature. If he had one.

He could see the brawny figure through the window. A large white napkin tucked under his collar. Rosa had said wait until he was well into his meal. He watched several mouthfuls disappear and then steeling himself, entered. With three strides he was at the table. The diner looked up in surprise. He swallowed hastily as his visitor sat down. Henrietta's bodyguard had been briefed by Rosa on mafia etiquette. He kept both hands on the table and his open jacket revealed no bulge under the armpit. He introduced himself slowly and carefully and explained his mission. To prevent bloodshed. He was surprised how even his voice was. There was no immediate reply. He sensed a pair of cold

181

blue eyes studying him. He felt the tension. It was broken by the arrival of Linda. Rosa was not stupid. He chose carbonara as ordered. It brought a nod of approval from Bambini. Both men admired her ample figure as she leaned over with her pad. Her neckline was lower than usual. Much lower. It introduced a further feeling of camaraderie. The Italian continued to eat but said nothing. His guest's food arrived and he started eating too. He again felt his adversary's eyes on him. He sensed they contained a mixture of contempt and pity.

"You are finding your task is difficult eh?" he asked. "We Italians are more skilful in these situations." He examined his fingers. "You have to know how to use your hands. The grip. That is most important. Too loose and they can escape. And we don't want that, do we my friend? Then we would have to start all over again."

The detective felt a stab of unease. He did not like these mind games. What was Bambini saying? That he was better at unarmed combat? If it was a psychological ploy it would not work. "I can handle myself as well as you," he replied stiffly.

The Italian's voice softened. "There is no need for bravado. Here, let show you." Leaning across, he took the detective's fork and picked up an unused spoon. Then deftly spinning the spaghetti against it, produced the perfect mouthful. His companion who had already had to wipe his chin twice, felt a wave of relief. So that was what he was on about. He nodded in appreciation. He tried it himself and found it easier.

"Good, good my friend," came the voice from across the table. "It is difficult for the English."

A frustrated Rosa, crouching by the door, could only hear the scrape of forks on plates. Finally the Italian laid down his and wiped his lips with his napkin. There was a certain warmth in his tone. "Food first, eh?"

Picking up a carafe of wine, he filled two glasses. It was a deep red. Very fitting, thought the detective, the colour of blood. The pourer leaned his elbows on the table. "So what you want?"

"Miss Tobias's life."

There came a sigh. "You ask the impossible my friend. She is already dead. It is ordained." He spread his arms wide. "As we say in Naples, she will sleep with the fishes."

But we're miles inland, thought his listener. Unless the idea was to dump her in the village pond. He pictured it. The ducks certainly wouldn't like that. He tried again. "Why has she got to die?"

"It is a matter of honour."

"You mean she made a fool of you."

The Italian's face darkened. "You be careful my friend. Very careful."

The detective knew sudden movement was dangerous. Otherwise he would have kicked himself. He had stupidly put a chill on a genial atmosphere. And after promising Rosa he would not make Bambini angry. Yet that was exactly what he had done. And after only five minutes. He was far better at stakeouts than negotiating. But what was there to negotiate? He could offer nothing in return for Henrietta's continued existence. At least nothing that would match the assassin's satisfaction at seeing her lifeless body. An idea began to from in his head. What if he could produce it for him? It was worth a try. After all, the villagers wanted her out of the way. And Bambini was well aware of that.

It was a case of manners. If he, as a foreigner, wanted to murder somebody in Italy, he would ask the locals to do it. He would never dream of invading their patch. And it should be the same in England. Bambini could sit back with a glass of wine while the deed was being done. With all the trouble Henrietta had caused, they would be no lack of volunteers. Then he would be given a photograph of the corpse. A decent sized one in colour which he could frame.

The Italian turned the offer over in his mind. Killing by proxy was not unknown. But he was not a fan. You had to hear the last choking cry. Watch the eyes glaze over. See the spurt of blood. And a photograph? No, he would have to inspect the body. Prod it. To make sure he was not being tricked. He recalled his motto. Nobody bamboozles Bambini. But he'd been shaken badly by his error over the Mother Superior. Maybe it was a possibility. Heavy lines of concentration appeared on his forehead. If he let them do it, he must receive decent consolation. It was only fair if he was missing the fun. A memento. He would need a memento to take home.

He leaned forward. "What you say is reasonable my friend and I am a reasonable man. You may dispose of her as you will but for Bambini a present. A finger or an ear. For the jar on my shelf."

Mr Chambers paled. He hadn't expected this. He couldn't imagine Miss Tobias giving up a finger for any plot. Especially the one which helped her to write her letters. Or going round with one ear. You could no longer hear people talking on either side of you. Faking death was one thing. Hacking bits off to give a would-be assassin was quite another.

"Our Church would not allow us to desecrate a body."

The Italian shrugged his shoulders. "So it is no deal."

"Would a blood stained blouse do?"

"It has to be flesh."

The detective could see they were getting nowhere. And there was no point in being evasive.

"We would have to bury all of her or none at all," he declared. "We can't have different parts of her in England and Italy."

Bambini grimaced. "What is a body? It is the soul that goes to heaven."

Not you though, thought his companion. He couldn't believe what was going on. Here they were in a quiet English village discussing dismembering a missionary. And however bizarre the conversation, it was deadly serious. Of Bambini's intentions he had no doubt. The man was a cold bloodied killer. He watched him slice a piece of cheese. He held the knife as if it was his dearest friend. One with a sharper blade could soon be plunging into Henrietta. He glanced round the room in despair. What else could he do? The Italian was not one to compromise. And pretending to kill his victim would never have a realistic chance of success. So there would be a physical showdown after all. And according to Rosa, Antonio's cousin had an impressive array of weapons. And what did he have? A knuckle duster. A gift from a boxer for helping find his stolen gloves. If it came to it, he wondered if he'd get close enough to swing a punch. The bristly jaw looked a good target.

Bambini appeared to read his thoughts. "So my friend, you have nothing more to offer. Now you are planning her protection."

"It is my duty."

"Many people have fallen in the line of duty."

"And many have not."

The Italian's gaze was like ice. "And which will be your fate?"

"Time will tell."

"And that time is coming."

"I know."

It was Bambini's turn to make a conciliatory effort. He did not want another obstacle in his way. "Look my friend, I have no quarrel with you. It is with that woman. She makes trouble for everyone. We can join forces. She trusts you. You keep her talking while I creep up behind. Then -."

He pulled a finger dramatically across his throat. The detective winced. He was glad the missionary was not listening to this. She was a formidable figure but her nerves were badly frayed. The Italian's presence had already made her faint once. And at that time he'd had no intention of murdering her. Now he could not wait to send her into the next world. Whatever that was. He'd often wondered what happened when you died. And if he barred Bambini's way, he might find out much earlier than he intended to. He could see no point in continuing the conversation. Nobody's mind was going to be changed on either side.

He stood up and mustering his friendliest tone, said. "I hope our paths do not cross. But if they do, may the best man win."

His listener looked confused.

"It's what we say in England. It's to show it's a sporting contest. You know, full of fair play."

Bambini could not believe what he was hearing. Fair play? With difficulty he suppressed a laugh. Wait until his mafia friends heard about this. If that was his opponent's attitude, it was going to be a piece of cake. Or, as they say in Naples, a slice of panettone. Play as dirty as you can. That was what his grandmother always stressed. Never do in daylight what you can do in the dark. And never do in the front what you can do at the back. And if you have to face the enemy, promise eternal friendship then pull the trigger. Simple rules to guide you through a carefree life. He got to his feet too. Never let the opposition tower over you. That was another adage he had to remember.

The detective surreptitiously stood on his toes to

make the most of his three inch advantage but felt anything but intimidating. He knew the die was cast. The Italian already seemed to be flexing his muscles for the coming contest. The Englishmen extended his hand for politeness. Bambini took it in a vice like grip. It tingled as he let it go. He did not want to rub it in front of his adversary. It would make him feel he had the edge. He put it in his pocket while the blood flowed back into his fingers. The Italian's face was etched in stone. "Until tomorrow my friend. We must waste no more time. I know your Miss Tobias. She will not run away. I shall come to the cottage in the morning. I wish you both sweet dreams."

Mr Chambers found himself out in the fresh air. He took several gulps. He needed it. Despite the warmth of the restaurant, it had been a chilling encounter. Bambini was indeed like a robot. Nothing was going to stop him.

The detective's brain was in turmoil. Should he call the police? It seemed a sensible idea. But what could he say? The truth was so preposterous they would laugh at him. They certainly wouldn't come out on his say so. They would put him down as a nutter. And that's what he was for allowing himself to get in such a position. They would apologise after Henrietta was dead but it would be too late then. He made his way slowly through the village. What was he going to tell her? He realised any plea to flee would fall on deaf ears. She had an appointment at the convent to hear the interviews. And nothing would deter her from keeping that. There was only one thing for it. They would have to barricade themselves in. He knew Mavis didn't like her furniture being even an inch out of place but this was an emergency. It was a stone building so Bambini could hardly set fire to it.

He pulled himself together. If he started to panic, it

would spread to the others. He had to put on a show of confidence. He started to whistle. That was better. The Italian wouldn't be without nerves either. He might give the impression of being ice cool but his heart would be pumping away inside just like theirs. That was if he had one. The lights of the cottage beckoned. This time he would remember the code. His hand had stopped tingling. And he was pleased to note as he started to knock, it did not shake.

Rosa at the keyhole had managed to hear enough. And she did not waste a second. For once in his life, Antonio would have to act. And in response to her urgent pleading he did. He called an emergency meeting of the conspirators. Only this time they must plan to save the missionary. Whatever she had done, did not deserve a death sentence.

It was nearly ten o'clock by the time everybody was gathered. The restaurant had been kept closed. The new arrivals settled round the tables while their host distributed carafes of his house red. It was an occasion which demanded a glass in the hand. Ant tended to be dramatic, but this time he did not need to overdo it. The atmosphere was grim as he reiterated what his wife had heard. He kept his voice low because his cousin was in his room on the other side of the kitchen. Yet such was the rapt attention, his hushed tones reached every straining ear. After he had finished, there was silence. The enormity of what was about to happen was slowly sinking into each worried brain.

The vicar was the first to speak. "In this situation we should start with a prayer. Please put your hands together." Falling to his knees, he began. "Oh Lord, we humbly beseech thee, have mercy on Miss Tobias's soul - "

"Hang on," said the newsagent. "I don't want to interrupt God's words, but she's not dead yet. It's setting completely the wrong tone."

"One cannot be too careful," rejoined Ronnie. "It's better than a hurried refrain afterwards."

"Never mind his words," retorted Angela, "what are we going to do?"

"Well, it's a bit awkward isn't it?" said James.

"What do you mean?"

"If Rosa's right, he'll set off about ten o'clock after he's had his lie in. I'll be opening the pub then."

"And I'll be taking choir practice," added the vicar.

"And there'll be a queue at the post office," said Arthur. "It's pension day."

"And I can hardly cancel surgery," put in the doctor, determined not to be left out. Or rather, left in.

"I'm sorry to have to join the club," ventured the colonel who felt likewise. "But I've promised to help Jenkins take our hens to market. They're very tricky to round up."

"So we're just going to let her get murdered," declared Angela who could hardly believe her ears.

"It won't come to that," replied James. "He's all talk. He couldn't even smuggle her into Italy. And then he pulled out of strangling that Mother Superior."

"Maybe that was a practice," said Arthur. "He could have been looking on his cord like a car engine. If you don't use it for a while, you need to check it's still in working order."

"It was no practice," stressed the restaurateur's wife who was being allowed to attend. "He stopped because he'd got the wrong person. We all know he was after Miss Tobias."

"I'm still convinced he's only out to frighten her," said the landlord. "But if we stand in his way, it will put him on his mettle. Once his blood is up, he may well go over the top. And then we would be to blame."

"It's up already," warned Rosa. "It's near boiling

point."

"It's not as if she's alone," pointed out George. "She's got that detective fellow and Mrs Pitts."

"What can they do against a professional killer," demanded the newsagent's wife.

"It's still three against one."

"It could be a dozen against one if you'd stand up to be counted. You're all craven cowards."

"That's a bit strong," said the colonel in an injured tone. "It's a case of standing back and coolly weighing up all the options."

"Well, you're certainly standing back."

He ignored the remark. "James is right. We must be careful not to inflame the situation. It is certainly an uncomfortable one for the missionary. But I seriously doubt that it will turn out to be fatal. I think we should adopt a watching brief. Keep an eye on him."

"And hope for the best," said Angela angrily.

"Of course we all hope for the best. And I am sure it will be realised."

"So you are doing nothing?" asked Rosa.

"A watching brief is not doing nothing. It will enable us to act at the last minute if necessary."

"Like trying to resuscitate her," said the newsagent's wife.

"Well actually," cut in the vicar, "the doctor is very good at that. Remember Mrs Adams. She was absolutely stone cold."

"Wait a minute," James suddenly exclaimed. "It's not up to us. We've got the law here."

Constable Tompkins shifted uncomfortably. He'd been trying to keep a low profile and was sitting well back by the cutlery boxes.

"You're right," agreed Arthur. "It's for Terry to stamp out violence."

"You cannot stamp it out until it's taken place,"

came the swift rejoinder. "I can't arrest him until he acts. It's not illegal to walk down the street."

"It is if he's going to murder somebody," put in the colonel.

"But we don't know that for sure," replied PC 42. "It's rumour, gossip, hot air. We just don't know."

The newsagent eyed him directly. "So you're not going to do anything."

"I didn't say that. I'll be around. Waiting to pounce if necessary. Like you've already said, keeping a watching brief."

James was not impressed. "From what distance?"

"As close as the regulations allow."

"What do you mean?"

"Police rule number one is not to intimidate the public. No heavy presence. So I won't be breathing down his neck. But on hand."

"Round about," said Arthur.

"Not round about. On hand."

Ant began collecting the glasses. He could see nobody was going to take any action. He noticed Rosa's bosom was beginning to heave with indignation. A bad sign. It was going to be a long night. As it certainly would be, he reflected, at the cottage. He watched the conspirators troop out in single file. Hardly a commando patrol. But who could blame them? They had no experience of the mafia. They did not believe that Bambini could be serious.

191

Chapter 40

The Mother Superior awoke on her second morning in a florist's shop. At least that's where she thought she was. Her bed was completely surrounded by flowers. They were on her windowsill, her beside table and the mantelpiece. All jostling to catch the early morning sun in a blaze of colour. The hedgerows and woods around the convent had been almost picked clean by the nuns. There were even some plastic carnations Sister Martina had found in a cupboard and put at the back. After a wash and an iron, you could not tell them apart.

The patient was not stupid. She knew she had to harden her heart. But this VIP treatment was having an effect. She could not deny it. She felt an increasing warmness towards the Reverend Mother. She had a certain style. Whether on the Lord's path or veering off it. Her mind went back to last night. Being lulled to sleep by the choir serenading her under the window. How had they chosen her three favourite psalms? Sister Martina must have rung her office but what about that extra one? All about forgiveness? Not very subtle. And it seemed to be sung with more feeling. But she'd listened to the words. And speaking of words, her throat was not so sore. She tried a murmur. It came out almost painlessly. She would be fit enough for the investigation tomorrow. In the meantime she would keep mum and continue to regain her strength.

There were soft footsteps in the corridor. Sister Martina entered bearing a tray. The herbal tea was steaming in its cup. Just as she'd ordered it the previous evening when offered a vast choice including red bush and Earl Grey. Her slice of fresh bread was soft and thin enough to be swallowed easily. It was nicely buttered and cut diagonally as she liked. The crusts were thoughtfully missing. Sister Martina's smile was as warm and welcoming as the geraniums in a glass by her elbow. If she preferred the floral tributes to be in the shape of wreaths, it did not show. She puffed up an already perfectly plump pillow as the Mother Superior nodded her 'good morning.' Then after carefully checking the room's temperature, she opened the window to allow in a little fresh air. With it came two dancing butterflies drawn by the perfume from the array of vases. The peacock and red admiral fluttered delightfully in tandem from one pot to another to the pleasure of the Mother Superior. She would not have been surprised if Sister Martina had organised their arrival too. Nothing appeared beyond her. Propped up to eat her breakfast, the patient had a good view of the lawn. She wondered on which spot the harrowing deed had taken place. The grass looked rather coarse. It must have been ticklish for whoever was cavorting there. She gave a sudden start which almost spilled her cup. What on earth was she thinking of? She admonished herself sharply. Idle thoughts of such nature were not allowed. And that decided her on how to spend the day. She might be lying in bed, but it would not be wasted. She wrote down a request for the file of everybody to be interviewed. She would do some psychoanalysing of their profiles. That's what Scotland Yard did with suspects in baffling cases. And there were none more baffling than this. A close study might provide an inkling of who had given in to that most popular of human weaknesses.

She had been tempted once herself as a seventeen year-old at school. It was just before she gave her life to the Church. Her geography teacher had sensibly pointed out she should test her desires before making a decision. And being on hand, kindly offered to help. Despite the cramped conditions in the broom cupboard, she was in real danger of failing when the bell went for rounders. It had gone off five minutes early and she was convinced it was God who had rung it. But that had been a long, long time ago. Since then she had devoted herself to her all seeing Master. She wondered what he thought of these goings on. He would have had a grandstand seat.

Sister Martina hurried off to do her bidding. Fortunately the records were kept in binders so the odd page could be removed if necessary. Her mind ran over the plan for the rest of the day. The patient would have a delicious chicken broth for lunch with fresh parsley sprinkled on it. Then to interrupt her analysing, a group of nuns would gather round her bed to read aloud parables. Especially chosen for their themes of giving sinners a second chance. Supper would be softly poached salmon which was true. It had been a present from Len the local countryman who was awaiting an appointment with Sister Adela when the coast was clear. That would be followed by a strawberry mouse and a mug of Ovaltine heavily laced with a sleeping drug. Hopefully the Mother Superior would not wake until the next afternoon. And then not be sure where she was. Delay was everything. The fly in the ointment was the missionary. It was comforting to know Bambini was after her, but so far he'd been distressingly unreliable.

Chapter 41

The inhabitants of the cottage barely slept that night. Mr Chambers dropped off for twenty minutes but wished he hadn't. His dream was full of threatening Italians bearing all sorts of weapons. When he produced his knuckle duster they'd shaken with laughter before circling closer. Luckily he woke up before they did him in.

He'd returned from meeting Bambini determined to produce an air of optimism. But once his failure became known, it evaporated as quickly as snowflakes in an oven. At one stage Henrietta and Mavis went round holding hands. That's how bad the atmosphere was. Then they had argued over what furniture to pile against the door. The cleaner wished she'd had everything valued so it could be the cheapest. The detective said the pieces had to be the heaviest. Nobody felt like breakfast but they were aware a successful army marches on its stomach. Even if this one had only three members and they weren't going anywhere. So they forced down a boiled egg each and two rounds of toast. Cracking his shell, Henrietta's bodyguard thought of Humpty Dumpty. He doubted if all the king's horses and all the king's men, could ever put their trio together again after the Italian's visit. He kept this scenario to himself as he surveyed the pale faces beside him. He looked at the clock on the wall. Nine o'clock. He imagined Bambini getting up. His muscles rippling as he stretched. He was unlikely to have much of a lie in today. It must be difficult to relax when full of murderous thoughts. He wondered what he would have for breakfast. Plenty of carbohydrates for energy. Then cool as a cucumber, he would step into the street and set off unerringly for the cottage. It was only a short distance. What would be thinking of on the way? The detective decided not to imagine that. There was no point in frightening yourself further. Or your companions. He tried again to put on a bold front. "Bambini's only just over five foot tall. He's not a giant."

"Size doesn't count in this case," replied the missionary. "Think of David and Goliath. We must outwit him. And be brave enough to do it. Mind over matter."

He could only admire her stance. Her sangfroid. It must be her faith. Her unwavering belief in her mission. It was what the old martyrs had. Joan of Arc could never have braved the stake without it. It was very impressive. But then Henrietta somewhat spoilt her image by spending twenty minutes in the lavatory. In the end, Mavis had to bang on the door and ask if she was all right. It was no good hiding there, it would be the first place the killer would look.

The detective stared out of the window. It was as if nature was setting the scene. The early sun had disappeared. Black clouds were rolling in from the west as if heralding the coming storm. These were being carried by an increasingly fresh breeze. This would be at Bambini's back. It would make his journey to the cottage even quicker. Mr Chambers shuddered. And not just because of the cold air. Sometimes in life, a man had to do what a man had to do. And in this case, any sensible one would flee. But the door was already barricaded. He settled down to watch the end of the street. That was where the squat and intimidating figure would first appear.

Chapter 42

A thunderous chorus of 'Valerie' came from the bathroom. Bambini was singing his battle song. It expanded his lungs and helped fine tune his body. He had ordered three different cheeses for breakfast. The most pungent in his cousin's larder. He gave his deodorant bottle a vigorous shake. He would be an exciting mixture of aromas. His armpits would smell of roses while his breath would conjure up a dragon's lair. He made a mental note to add a clove of raw garlic. It was not a day for half measures. He dressed carefully having opted for the Mussolini look. Black sweater, black shirt, black trousers, black socks, black shoes. But no black tie. That could only be worn after the killing. Otherwise it would be too patronising. Taking things for granted. Not that there was any doubt about the outcome. OK, that bodyguard was a couple of inches taller. But where was the trim, hard figure? He'd noticed him wobbling when he entered the restaurant. He was all flab. He deserved credit for seeking a confrontation. Yet he'd left a snivelling wreck. All it had taken was a handshake. He wished now he'd pumped his arm up and down as well. That really would have done the trick.

Sitting at the kitchen table, he tucked a large napkin under his chin. You didn't go on a mission with bits of food down your front. Rosa watched impassively as he chewed his way through the mountain on his plate. There was no sign of Antonio. He had found it convenient to clear out the attic which had needed doing for three years. Finishing his last mouthful, his cousin returned to his room. From there came the sound of humming. Rosa tiptoed to the door which was ajar. Peeping in, she saw his three weapons neatly laid out on the bed. The pistol and the knife flanked the cord with small spaces in between. Bambini began to chant as his finger darted from one to the other. "Enio, menio, minio, mo, catch a victim by her toe. If she hollows, kill her slow, enio, menio, minio, mo."

It was the last stage. The assassin was choosing his tool of death. She did not wait to see the outcome. She hurried out into the street. Yes, the chalk mark was there. She had put on her long sight glasses and it was clearly visible. She felt butterflies in her stomach but consoled herself that at least half the village would be feeling the same.

Bambini appeared in the doorway. He sensed all eyes were on him. And he was not wrong. The doctor was peering across the road from the safety of his surgery. And the landlord and the vicar were watching from the sanctuary of the Nag's Head's main bar. Even up the hill, the colonel was training his binoculars on the scene from the second floor landing. Only the newsagent behind his counter could not see, but his wife was giving him a running commentary from the spare bedroom via the back stairs.

The Italian rolled his shoulders like a boxer entering the ring. But now of course, the gloves were off. Slowly he bent his knees. Good, everything was circulating normally. He was at peak fitness. Straightening, he slowly looked around. He caught sight of the half hidden pale faced onlookers. He allowed himself a brief smile. They had made a wise decision. He had inhabited a ghost town. The street was empty. As he stepped out, Rosa appeared from a side door ten yards to the rear. She looked in vain for constable Tompkins. Where was he? He had promised to be a restraining presence. He later explained he had been delayed by a troublesome shoelace.

Bambini began to stride purposefully forwards.

Rosa followed silently at his heels. She noticed the gun and the knife in his belt and the cord dangling from his pocket. That 'enio, menio, minio, mo' rarely worked. It would be a late, late choice again. If he was allowed to make it. She pushed everything from her mind and began desperately to concentrate. She could see the chalk mark on the post office wall. In one stride he would reach it. There had to be perfect timing.

"Bambini," she shouted with all the power she could muster. Her always strident voice seemed to rebound off the surrounding walls. Several pigeons on a telephone wire nearly fell off in fright. The Italian stopped and turned on the spot. As he did so, Angela leaned out of the open window above and removed the peg holding her hanging basket. The lobelia, both white and blue and tastefully arranged, plummeted downwards in their wooden container. There's a popular saying an accident victim 'didn't know what hit him.' In Bambini's case it was perfectly true. When he came round, he thought he'd been struck by lightning. He was later to rue once more failing to heed his grandmother's words. An enemy can attack from any direction.

As he lay unconscious, spread-eagled on the pavement, a crowd swiftly gathered. George appeared carrying his medical case. "Let me through," he demanded. "I'm a doctor." Everybody knew that. But they instantly made a channel like the parting of the Red Sea. Kneeling, he gently pushed up the victim's eyelids. The normally penetrating pupils had glazed over. The face wore a surprised expression with the mouth hanging open. The ministering angel was forced to turn briefly away. He'd dealt with many cases of bad breath, but this was ridiculous. Feeling with his practised fingers, he checked the Italian's heart. It was keeping a steady beat. It was the head which caused the main concern. It did look a bit square. But that was because the hair was flattened. There was no sign of blood.

"He will live," pronounced the crouched figure getting stiffly to his feet. "But we must get him to hospital. He will need x-rays."

Rosa had already rung for an ambulance. She did not want to be his executioner. Even for the best of reasons.

As it arrived, so did PC 42. Taking the piece of chalk from her, he waved the crew back. It would only take a second. Stooping low, he drew an outline round the prostrate figure.

"I thought you only did that at crime scenes," said the vicar. "This was an accident."

"I know, but it's got to be official. I expect Health and Safety will be sticking their noses in. No doubt all these hanging baskets will be banned."

"Well, it's a small price to pay for saving the missionary's life."

"Don't worry. I was poised to act if things got out of hand. I was all set when the flower pot fell. He would have had to face me before he got to the cottage."

"But you said you couldn't do anything until he acted."

"I could see he was armed. That's intent. Like burglars carrying screwdrivers." He picked up the weapons. "I'd better take these into custody. We don't want them going to hospital. There could be awkward questions." He put them in his helmet. "As it is, it's an unfortunate mishap. A rotten peg and being in the wrong place at the wrong time. It could happen to anybody."

They watched the inert Italian being loaded into the back of the vehicle. The doors closed and he was gone. The atmosphere lightened with every yard it sped away.

James said what everybody was thinking. "I suggest a little drink to celebrate."

After calling the ambulance, Rosa had rung the cottage. Soon three relieved figures arrived to join the party along with the colonel who had sprinted down the hill. Henrietta had only been in the pub once before. When she had first bearded constable Tompkins. This time her step was much lighter. Although she firmly refused anything stronger than lemonade. Mavis ordered a large sweet sherry but kept her hand clasped round the glass so nobody could see how much was in it. The detective stuck to beer but the pints were sinking fast. He proudly produced his knuckle duster. That would have fitted perfectly on Bambini's chin; an equally effective knockout. But frustratingly the hanging basket had spoilt his chance. He shrugged his shoulders. One had to be sporting and accept the fact. The colonel had forced himself to stay up the hill to get a better overall picture. That's what commanders in the field did. But he would have been at the cottage in a trice. He'd even left his front door open ready to quicken his journey. The vicar and the landlord stressed that they too, had been in their starting blocks. They were both ex rugby players and if necessary, would have brought the Italian down with flying tackles at the cottage gate. Even Arthur who was committed to manning the post office counter, had been itching for action. He could hardly sit still and had twice stamped the wrong form.

Rosa and Angela listened to this outburst of heroism with mounting scorn. If it hadn't been for them, Miss Tobias could well be dead. As to rushing to her side, most of these boasters would not have made it in time for her funeral.

"I think this shows the women of Hatchett will always be safe," declared George, who though professionally unable to indulge in violence, was proud to have been first to reach the battlefield.

This was all too much for the newsagent's wife. "So which of you actually lifted a finger?" she demanded, standing hands on hips. "Not a single one. What a lot of big brave men you are. All you do is huff and puff. You should be ashamed of yourselves. Leaving it all to two helpless females."

"I must protest," replied the colonel, fingering his regimental tie. "Yours was the most foolhardy act saved by a lucky strike. What would have happened if you'd missed? It could have put him in a blind rage. He might have murdered half the village. Where would we be then?"

"You would still be on top of the hill."

The military figure ignored this. "History is littered with precipitous actions which have brought disaster. The charge of the Light Brigade and going over the top on the Somme. Those are two prime examples. You must husband your resources. Bide your time. Then at the precise moment - ."

Angela's eyes flashed. "Your precise moments never come. And that's the danger. Do you think Bambini's finished? He'll come out of hospital with such a headache he will want to murder the whole of Hatchett."

Rosa stepped in to calm things down. "I promise he will not try again."

James stared at her in disbelief. "How can you be so sure?"

"I know Antonio's cousin. Leave everything to me."

The vicar took advantage of the stunned silence. He pictured himself in the pulpit. "We must uplift our hearts. We are here to celebrate not argue. A cloud has been driven from the horizon."

Several of his temporary congregation murmured

their agreement. But they were thinking of the other cloud. The one clutching the lemonade glass. The one they would equally liked dispersed. And the sooner the better.

He appeared to read their thoughts. "There is one amongst us who has caused much angst and gnashing of teeth. But we are all Christians and extend the hand of friendship. We must now live together in harmony. Yet," he went on hurriedly, "if Miss Tobias was sent to show us the error of our ways, her job is done. And we wish her God speed to her next destination."

Henrietta imagined herself in a jungle clearing surrounded by heathens. For that is what this motley collection were. True, the smoking club had been disbanded, the cars were parked properly, and the obscene videos were no longer on display. But irreverence still beat in their hearts. If not, they would have confessed their all consuming sin. Fornicating at the convent. She felt like a sheriff of the old west. She had one last shoot out to face. And her draw would be quickest to defeat sister Martina and cleanse that den of iniquity. It was a cause she had never deviated from. If ever her determination wavered, she only had to shut her eyes. The vision was always there. That dreadful bottom bouncing irresponsibly; it's mysterious identity cruelly taunting her.

She sensed the onlookers awaiting a reply. She put down her glass. "Hatchett is returning to the path of righteousness" she declared. "But it is not there yet. The Lord is looking sorrowfully down on those transgressors who have yet to repent. I warn them that the day of reckoning is nigh. In fact tomorrow. The Mother Superior and I will bring to the attention of the world, the names of the sinners. And in particular, the one who barest his bottom to the heavens. Then indeed there will be much wailing and gnashing of teeth. And the guilty ones will seek to hide themselves." Her voice rose. "But it will be to no avail. Those that are married will be turned out of their homes. Their punishment will be a spell in the wilderness. There will be no early forgiveness. Only the almighty God will show mercy. But only to those who denounce their sins. So tonight, pray as you have never prayed before. Get down on your knees and clasp your hands. Otherwise the leaping flames of justice will scorch you."

PC 42 nudged Arthur. "She's much better than Ronnie. Twice the fire and brimstone. You couldn't fall asleep listening to her."

"Don't worry about that. They'll be a lot of wide awake people tonight. This really is zero hour."

"Do you think she'll pull it off?"

"It's in the lap of the gods."

"Hopefully not her one."

Chapter 43

Bambini opened his eyes. The dazzling white of the ward's ceiling was too bright to look at. He closed them again. His head was pounding like a thousand horses' hooves. He gingerly felt it with a finger. It was thickly swathed in bandages. His ears were free and he heard a door handle turn. Footsteps approached the bed. A gentle voice ordered "open wide." A nurse with a thermometer. He did as he was told. Something juicy was popped in. He bit it and felt a pip. He forced himself to look. As he did so, there was a vivid flash. Was it his brain? Then came another from over by the window. It was a camera. And holding it was Rosa. He sensed a nearer presence. Turning a little, he saw Henrietta leaning over him. She was poised with another grape. Rosa kept clicking, always keeping the Italian in the picture. Next, the missionary was putting blooms in a vase beside him. Then taking out a get well card, she read its contents aloud. "Dear Mr Bambini. As a helpless woman, I am so sorry to have put you in hospital. It was not a tactful thing to do. I trust it will not damage your reputation as a highly professional killer. But for future reference, a flower pot can match a gun, knife or cord. Best wishes for a speedy recovery. Henrietta."

"Miss Tobias is a committed Christian," said Rosa taking another picture of the patient's bandages. "She wants to apologise to the whole of Naples for your plight. So copies of her card together with these photographs will be sent to all leading newspapers. Their editors will like such a colourful story. They will put it on their front page and no doubt, will want to interview you."

The pounding inside Bambini's brain seemed to

increase tenfold. A wave of panic swept up and down his body. He tried to speak but no words come out. Had he been struck dumb with fright? Finally he made himself heard. "Rosa," he said, summoning up his most cajoling tone. "Why take the trouble? You are a busy woman." He would have spread his arms wide but they were pinned under the blankets. "It is only a little matter."

"Only a little matter? " replied Antonio's wife. "Trying to kill an innocent woman? What about those weapons?"

"It was only a joke."

"So it was only a joke, was it?"

"Yes, I just wanted to frighten her a little."

"So there is no vendetta?"

He shook his head and momentarily saw stars. "No, no. As I say, it was purely a little fun."

"And the fun is over?"

"Yes, yes."

"So when you get out of here, you will go straight back to Italy?"

"I give my word. On Toni's grave."

"Who's Toni?"

"My cat."

"What about your mother and father's?"

"They're still alive."

"If you go back on your promise, these will immediately go to the newspapers."

The Italian closed his eyes and imagined the disastrous scene. Naples's elite hit man lying prostrate in bed while his female victim pops grapes into his mouth. He grimaced and again saw stars. He knew when he was beaten, but luckily this was not happening in Italy. If they both kept their word, and he would certainly keep his, then this dreadful affair would stay secret. The only bright spot was his grandmother would never find out. He could not bear the thought of how her lip would curl.

He realised they were all watching him. The other person in the room by the wall was Mr Chambers. The detective felt a stab of sympathy for his adversary. Or rather ex adversary. They were in similar professions although his latest victim had been an annoying wasp in his office window. And that had taken two blows with his rolled up Daily Mail. Bambini was a prisoner of his own upbringing. Every wrong had to be avenged. However slight. He could understand how he felt finding rocks in the coffin. Nobody likes to be made a complete fool of. Especially when you have hot blood coursing through your veins. But it was all over now. He had made a promise and the detective was sure he would keep it. And anyway, he'd shown him how to eat spaghetti properly. He'd always be grateful for that. He stepped forward and shook the patient most cordially by the hand. The sight prompted Henrietta to kiss what was visible of the Italian's forehead. He flushed with embarrassment. Luckily Rosa was caught off guard and failed to take a picture. Be thankful for small mercies, he told himself.

Outside in the car park, the missionary said a second farewell. She no longer needed her bodyguard. Nor his detecting skill. Bambini was banished and tomorrow the mystery of the convent would be solved. Yet he had been a stalwart companion. A comforting figure in all her troubles. All right, she suspected he drank too much but then he didn't have her faith to sustain him. It would make a good sermon. The advantages of prayer over a bottle of whisky in times of stress. Or in some cases, several bottles. There were no hangovers with praying unless you concentrated too hard. She would certainly mention him in her next batch. He could do with a little guidance in that field.

The detective pocketed his last wad of notes. There was nothing like cash in hand. Although he doubted if his benefactor had any idea of the ways of the taxman. It had been quite an adventure. A bit nerve wracking at times but exhilarating. At least afterwards. He did not take to all this religion but he admired the missionary's sense of purpose. He knew his job was done but he had his own gift to make. He handed her an envelope. Inside were the contents of his burglary. The convent's secret code. He had kept it until the time was ripe. It would be Henrietta's sucker punch. She had forgotten it in her mounting excitement. She slipped it gratefully into her pocket. What could Sister Martina say to this? It would come out of the blue like a bombshell. She looked at the detective with shining eyes. It was the perfect ammunition for any firing squad. She could already see the Reverend Mother lined up against the wall. Her benefactor could sense it was going to be a dramatic finale. He wished he could have hung around for it. Oh to be a fly on the wall. Having been involved, he felt it right he should hear the outcome. And Mavis, who was equally keen herself, had promised to let him know. He had looked at the odds in Mrs Gardner's window. He felt it could be any of the front runners. So he'd kept his money in his pocket but he would spend a couple of quid raising a glass to the winner. If that was the right word. He could not think of a better way to become famous. Not that he would have chosen that path himself. It must have been chilly whatever the weather.

He dropped Henrietta and Antonio's wife outside the restaurant before heading home. At least his cat Button would be waiting to greet him. Unlike Bambini's Toni, stiff as a board in the deep freeze. The missionary clasped Rosa's hand as she said goodbye. She had been a friend of biblical proportions. She had more than made up for those villagers who had plotted against her. She told the detective the time had come for her to return to Africa. Her work in Hatchett would be finished tomorrow. She knew the hour had arrived because God had sent a message. Everybody's life was full of messages. The trick was to spot them. She had greatly admired the hanging baskets. They contained a multitude of different flowers. Yet it was the one with lobelia that had crashed down on Bambini. And lobelia was the name of the tribe she had lived with in the Congo. It was not a coincidence. It was a sign.

Rosa knew about her being tipped from a stretcher on her previous mission. After saving her life in Hatchett, she did not want her to be in danger again. She voiced her fears. The missionary nodded. Yes, she had thought of that too. She had been in touch with the local ambulance service. They had given her a booklet on the latest carrying techniques. As soon as she returned, she would start a course for the more able bodied men. It was really a case of commonsense. Of looking where you were going and not talking too much. The problem was, there were huge numbers of tree roots on jungle paths. The bearers were always tripping over them or thinking they were snakes. Especially if they had been smoking their hash. Rosa suggested a helmet like the one Norman wore. Henrietta appreciated the thought but said it would be far too hot.

She made her way back to the cottage where Mavis was waiting all agog. The missionary told her what had happened at the hospital. The danger was over. All she needed was a good night's sleep.

That of course was what Sister Martina intended for the Mother Superior, but she was thwarted. Her Ovaltine looked a little too thick and rich. A sniff and a sip confirmed her suspicions. A drug had been added to it. The patient had nearly been seduced by the wonderful hospitality but she had come to her senses in time. Once left alone, she tipped the drink into the basin. However she said not a word. Let the Reverend Mother think the plan had succeeded. She would be in for a big surprise in the morning. Several heads popped round the door. But on each occasion she had enough warning to shut her eyes and be breathing serenely.

Sister Martina had little time to spare for her patient during the remaining hours. She was making her own final preparations. Had her special parcel arrived yet? Yes, it had. Good. Was everybody ready for their interview? As far as they ever would be. In what she believed was a masterstroke, she had persuaded the Mother Superior that the nuns be seen in reverse alphabetical order. This was how the convent did it with interviews. First one way, then the other. It ensured that each had a fair share of waiting their turn. It meant that Sister Adela would be cross examined last. By that time, the interrogator might well have had enough. Those going before her had been instructed to play as dumb as possible. To string things out. This would be no hardship for several of them. Each was to ask to have a prayer said before the questions began. To give them the strength to answer crisply and clearly. One that should be repeated after the speaker. And in a manner hesitantly and slowly to show how much it was needed. And if possible, accompanied by a tear in the eye. The situation was enough to bring tears to anybody's eye. But the big question was, who would laugh last? The Reverend Mother was determined it would be her. Yet she was well aware her two adversaries had very different ideas. Her big advantage was she knew which nun they were after. They did not.

She summoned Sister Adela to her office. First things first. Her dress. This time instead of wearing a habit a size too small, it must be one too large. And there would be no last minute shower. Anything but. She should do knees ups and strenuous exercises just before her turn came. To get the perspiration going. It would help keep the Mother Superior at a distance. And not let her hair tumble down over her shoulders. It should be in the tightest and severest bun. And with streaks of grey. The speaker passed her a packet of dye. The young girl reacted with horror.

"Don't worry," the Reverend Mother assured her, "it will wash out. You can also experiment with ash for a slight moustache. There is plenty around the garden bonfire."

"You're turning me into an ogre."

"No, you're being interviewed by one."She took the young girl's hand. "Nature has endowed you with many assets. And on top of those, a willingness to please whoever you are with. You are unable to say 'no' and find it virtually impossible to tell a lie. In normal circumstances these would be excellent traits. But in this situation they are dangerous liabilities. Therefore we have to put the Mother Superior off from the start. Hopefully she will take one look and decide no man would fancy you. But if she persists, you know our last line of defence. If you have to tell an untruth, shut your eyes. That helps you stop looking guilty."

Sister Adela sounded close to despair."I don't think I can go through with this. I'm sure I'll let you down."

"Of course you won't," responded the Reverend Mother with more confidence than she felt. "See it as a one act play. it will be over in no time."

"The last show you put on was a complete disaster. And I can't climb over a wall and disappear. I'll be stuck here facing the music."

"The only music tomorrow will be the song in our hearts. I know we will succeed. Then you can get back to business. You've had a good rest."

Chapter 44

Bambini cut a pitiful figure in the departure lounge. His head still hurt if he moved it. So he kept it slumped on his chest. Downcast was not the word. He couldn't believe his fate. It seemed to be a dream. Or rather a nightmare. Yet the bandage was all too real. Solicitous airport staff had asked what had happened. He'd told them a road accident. You could hardly say you'd been floored by a flower pot could you? It was all so embarrassing. Especially if you were a ruthless killer. And who would be in Naples to greet him? He closed his eyes in horror. His grandmother. She loved to meet her conquering hero. Or in this case, conquered hero.

What could he tell her? The trouble was, she knew when he tried to have her on. Exaggerating. If he said he'd pumped six bullets into a victim, she'd instinctively know it was three. If he said he'd overcome a six foot bull of a man, she'd sense he was five foot ten and several stones lighter. If you looked her in the eye you'd had it. And if you averted your gaze, you'd had it too. It was like being in the dock. He'd always said she should be a judge. He counted up the mistakes he had made on the trip. Far too many. And she'd go through them one by one.

There was no way of avoiding her. But he would keep the hospital part out of it. He gave a involuntary shiver. He would never eat another grape. But how to explain the rest? He was attacked from behind. Well, from on top. A missile artfully camouflaged by flowers. It was a brilliant stroke of cunning. Anybody would have fallen for it. He gave a sudden frown. Anybody but Norman. He had seen the danger. He always wore a helmet. He posed as the village idiot but he was far from one. Only he had tracked down Bambini's secret firing range. The Italian's suspicions increased. Maybe he was the real mastermind. The one who had plotted his downfall. This could mean another vendetta. He'd promised to end the one against the missionary but there was nothing to stop him starting another. Yet he was not that stupid. The village should be treated with kid gloves. Palermo and Messina might brag about being dangerous places but they couldn't hold a candle to Hatchett. True they had plenty of flowers too. But these only appeared at funerals when they could no longer hurt the victims. He boarded the plane clutching a box of his grandmother's favourite chocolates. With a bit of luck, she wouldn't want to talk too much with her mouth full.

His hopes of slipping away in the jostling crowds were quickly dashed. Her cry of 'Bambini, Bambini' rose above the hubbub. He was engulfed in hugs. He thrust his present at her. She took it and dropped it unopened into her bag. "Which weapon did you use eh?" she asked eagerly. "I think the cord. It is quiet and clean. It is better suited for an English village."

Her grandson moistened his dry lips as she continued. "Did she gurgle good? Did she squirm?"

"No, she didn't."

"She just went limp eh?"

"She's still alive."

He received a startled stare.

"I had a message from above. It overwhelmed me."

"You mean in your head?"

"Well, more on it."

"So you were converted?"

"Yes. When I came round I knew I would not be able to kill her."

"When you came round?"

"The message was so strong it knocked me out. I had to lie down. For quite a while."

"So was she grateful?"

"Grateful?" He spread his hands wide. "Never was somebody so grateful. She fed me grapes, big juicy ones." He took her by the shoulders. "And do you know what? She wanted to thank me publicly. To put the story in our newspapers. But I said no, no, we mafia work in the shadows. I did right yes?"

"Of course." Her eyes suddenly narrowed. "What is this?"

Bambini had pulled his cap down low but one of his bruises still showed. "It was my anger."

"Anger?"

"Yes. I had shown weakness. So I kept banging my head against a wall to knock sense into it."

She took his arm sympathetically. "Come, we will go home. I don't think there is much inside for it to respond to."

Chapter 45

The sun came up on a perfect day. Not a breath of wind nor a cloud in the sky. Sister Martina's half hearted prayer for a raging storm or an earthquake had been ignored. She had instructed everybody in the convent to be extra quiet. To keep the Mother Superior sleeping for as long as possible. The drug was to be left to do its work. The instigator tiptoed down the corridor and put her head round the door. The bed was empty. At that moment the patient appeared outside the window. "Isn't it a lovely morning," she called. "I've just taken a turn round the grounds. I don't know how to thank you. I've got my voice and energy back."

The Reverend Mother somehow forced a smile. "That is good news" she said through almost gritted teeth. "I expect your walk has given you an hearty appetite." Now would be the last throw. A laxative in the cereal. Even this dedicated investigator wouldn't be desperate enough to conduct interviews through a lavatory door. "We have some excellent All Bran and fresh yoghurt."

"That's most kind. But I've already had two slices of toast and a poached egg. As the weather is so nice, I will conduct operations on the lawn. Nothing like being at the scene of the crime. It may help jog memories."

That was another blow for Sister Martina. The bright conditions might well show up Sister Adela's camouflage. She had just changed a sixty watt bulb for a forty in the room that should have been used. Nothing was going right so far. But she was good at keeping her nerve. The question was, could the young girl?

The one in question was staring into the mirror. She had the strange feeling she was looking at herself far into the future. She had overdone the dye and resembled a grandmother. It was too late to do anything about it now. But the moustache would have to go. It ran with the slightest perspiration. Sitting still, she was already feeling hot and bothered. She would not be needing many knees ups to be pongy.

Four chairs had been placed on the grass. One for the Mother Superior, one for Miss Tobias, one for the Reverend Mother, and one for the unfortunate being grilled. The nuns were to sit in a group waiting their turn to be called. Sister Martina had warned she would be marking their performance out of ten. Those that scored over seven would be let off evening prayers and allowed to watch her video of Dirty Dancing.

She went round her charges individually. A word of encouragement here, a pat on the shoulder there. No football manager could have done better to galvanise his team before a big match. And it was needed. The collective butterflies fluttering in their stomachs would have filled a forest glade. Although all were innocent apart from Sister Adela, they knew they had to protect her. They had each benefited from her special work. And like anybody used to a decent standard of living, they did not want to give it up. And they felt uncomfortable over being asked about men. As any self respecting nun would. Especially those who preferred girls. Which was most of them. They had promised the Reverend Mother they would not hold hands however great the pressure. They would sit with them demurely in their laps.

Henrietta arrived exactly at the appointed hour of ten. It had taken all her willpower not to come earlier. This was to be her moment of triumph. Her crowning glory. She too had long been out of bed. She had spent the first hour in meditation. This had been spoilt at a crucial moment by Mavis running a bath, but she had not complained. The cleaner had been a devoted companion. Even so, it had made her a little grumpy.

Her spirits were quickly restored when she met her Frenchman. At least he said he was French, although his accent occasionally seemed to slip. She'd feared he wouldn't turn up but he was ready and waiting for her. Gratitude poured from every pore at the sight of him. He was going to turn everything round at the very last minute. She'd found her saviour in the nearby town. She had seen his advertisement in the window. On impulse she had gone in. Yet later she realised of course it was divine guidance. Did clients have to come to him? Or did he go on assignments? Yes he did. In that case she had exactly the one for him. He'd failed to hide a grimace at what she'd proposed. This had made her think he might not appear, but he'd said he liked a challenge and they'd shaken hands on it.

He drove her to the convent in his battered Ford. She tried to make conversation but he asked her to keep quiet. He needed to marshal his thoughts. He agreed to wait in the background near the potting shed until she waved him forward. Greeting the Mother Superior, Henrietta took her aside and explained his presence. Sybil looked serious for a moment. It was not something a member of the Order should be subjected to. But if the worse came to the worse, he would be let loose.

The pair surveyed the cluster of pale faced nuns. No wonder they had lost their colour. The wrath of God was at hand. And the missionary was certain the Mother Superior would pass his anger on one hundred percent. And what about the owner of that naughty bottom somewhere in the village? How would he be feeling now? Everybody knew the die was being cast.

The three central figures took their seats. As they did so, Miss Tobias suddenly produced her envelope. "I think we should ask the nuns the meaning of this," she declared removing the precious piece of paper. "Or maybe the Reverend Mother can help?"

The recipient of this inquiry leaned forward. "What is it?"

"It is a secret code concerning the goings on at your convent. I am not at liberty to divulge how I got it. There are initials and times which I suggest relate to the names and the visits of what I would politely term clients."

Sister Martina conjured up a helpful look. "What are they?"

"I believe they are a record of the fateful day. A K.K. and an S.S. were here in the early afternoon. One came swiftly after the other." The speaker's voice betrayed a note of exaltation. "Please reveal their identities."

"What do you mean 'their'?" responded her listener perfectly calmly. "There is no 'their' at all. Those letters refer to lessons. We do not spend all our time at prayer."

The missionary looked confused. "Lessons?"

"Yes. K.K. stands for keen knitters. We have a large class. We are doing scarves for orphan children at the moment."

Henrietta felt the ground slipping away beneath her feet. "Well, what about S.S.?" she demanded.

"Secure sewers. We pride ourselves on never dropping a stitch. There's never a hole in our habits."

The Mother Superior interrupted impatiently. "Let us begin. We have wasted enough time already."

Miss Tobias subsided like a pricked balloon. But Sister Martina was in no mood to congratulate herself on a smart piece of thinking. They were not out of the woods yet. Not by a long chalk. More like still in thick forest.

Sister Jessica came forward first. She was a

forthright north country girl. She received a smile of encouragement from the Reverend Mother. She sat down with a groan on the edge of her chair. No, she did not like men. And if she did, she could do nothing about it in her condition. Her bad back had plagued her for months. Sister Martina had to suppress a giggle. She had played tennis with her the day before. Bravo. Full marks. She was gratified to note that Sister Rita who came next, had developed a limp. She had to perch gingerly with her leg stretched straight out before her. Hardly in a fit condition for fresh air hanky panky. Eight out of ten.

Slowly the queue was being whittled away. Sister Pauline who could hear a pin drop at ten yards, now found hearing difficult. She did not want to change the subject but could a flag be waved at praying time? She could no longer hear the bell. Every question had to be repeated several times. The Mother Superior felt herself going hoarse. Her throat was delicate enough as it was. The missionary tapped her foot in frustration. She seemed to be the only one with everything in working order. She sensed they were being given the run-around. Again. And Sybil appeared oblivious to it. But she was not. She knew a delaying tactic when she saw one. Well, nobody was going to grind her down. She would turn it to her own advantage. The longer the proceedings took, the more frayed the nerves of the real culprit would be. She called for an adjournment for lunch.

They all trooped inside for salad and cheese rolls. The Mother Superior watched the diners carefully. Those that had already been interrogated, munched away happily. Those yet to come, had markedly less appetite. One in particular, ate virtually nothing. Barely pecking at a solitary slice of cucumber. She wore a loose fitting garment and had grey hair. Although none of the nuns were animated, she was decidedly listless. She would be the one to watch.

The interviews continued. And as one after the other successfully passed, Sister Martina saw the flaw in her plan. If nobody had been fingered by the time Sister Adela's turn came, she would be the obvious suspect. It was too late to change the order. She could only sit helplessly and watch the drama unfold.

It was two o'clock when at last the young girl was called. The sun beat down from almost overhead. It shone straight into her eyes. There was no need for a Gestapo lamp. Sister Adela settled herself. She felt three pairs of eyes on her. One sympathetic, two hostile and probing. The previous three or four victims had lacked the flair of the earlier ones. They seemed short of breath and almost in a faint. The Mother Superior had feared she was being too hard but experience told her to keep up the pressure. Now she had the last rabbit in her unwavering headlights. Her voice had an edge it had not had before. "Do you like men?"

The young girl found herself answering too swiftly and too easily. "Yes."

"Please expand your answer."

"I have nothing against them. The ones I have met have been kind and friendly."

"And where did you see them?"

"In the village. When I went shopping."

"And never at the convent?"

"Sometimes, yes. When they came on business delivering things."

The interrogator decided to change tack.

"Do you ever spend time relaxing on the lawn?"

"Yes. We all do in fine weather."

"Always with female company?"

"Yes."

"Are you sure?"

"I think so."

"What does that mean?"

"Well, not completely."

"Exactly. I put to you on a certain date in April you were with a male figure."

"I can't remember dates but it's possible."

"Do you know the name of this companion?"

Sister Martina found the Lord's prayer was on her lips. If it was true he forgave sinners, now was the time to show it. He had let them down once over the National Lottery. That was fair enough. They had been greedy. But having the wrong numbers had led to this situation. So it was partly his fault.

Sister Adela's voice interrupted her reverie. "Yes I do."

"Then child, what is it?"

The atmosphere was electric. Henrietta could hear her heart thumping. The Reverend Mother had forsaken asking for mercy and had her fingers crossed.

"Henry. That's what I call him."

The face of every man the missionary knew in Hatchett, flashed before her. None was known by that name. She could not help herself. She was only an observer but had to speak. "Where is he? Where does he come from?"

"Yes, where does he come from?" echoed the Mother Superior.

"Do you want to meet him?"

"Yes," chorused the pair.

"He is waiting in my room."

Whatever their feelings, both felt a surge of admiration for the transgressor. He had come to own up. To face the music. Not for him skulking in the shadows. Mind you, thought Henrietta, he certainly likes doing things in the open.

The Mother Superior recovered herself first. "Then

bring him here."

It was the missionary's turn to produce an echo. "Yes, yes, bring him here."

As if on cue, two nuns emerged from the living quarters. Between them they supported a male figure. It was naked. The two onlookers caught their breath. But as it came closer, they realised what it was. A blow up doll. The Mother Superior's brain was ice cold. So that's why those nuns had appeared looking exhausted. They had spent their lunch break puffing lungfuls of air into it.

Her voice betrayed no hint of a surprise as she turned to the young girl. "So this is your companion?"

"Yes."

"And you play with it on the lawn?"

"My bed is too narrow."

Henrietta did not believe a word of what was being said. But as the rubber apparition was set down before her, she saw that indeed it sported a pimple. Sister Martina read her thoughts. "They're made to order these days. You can have a birthmark, a wart, even carbuncles. The last are popular because they give you more of a grip."

Miss Tobias felt she should be getting a grip. She had to hand it to the manufacturers. It was very lifelike. But she saw what she saw. Only flesh and blood could produce such a vibrant bouncing display. However clever Sister Adela claimed to be at manipulating it.

Now was the time to introduce her ace card. She nodded to Sybil who made the shock announcement. "We know Sister Adela has nothing to hide. So she will be happy to undergo hypnotism. It is a great help to remembering things that may have been genuinely forgotten. There could more than a doll involved." She turned to the Reverend Mother. "You have no objection?"

Sister Martina had just sent a nun hastening to the stationary cupboard. "None at all. I'm certain it will be most constructive."

A path was cleared for Pierre le Stare. He was a small man with dark hair and as you would expect, penetrating eyes. He positioned himself immediately in front of his victim and gave her a reassuring smile. He asked her to clear her mind as he would do his. They were partners together going on a journey back in time. In this interval, Sister Martina assisted the young girl to settle and slipped the result of the errand into her hand. Her fingers closed over a drawing pin. The sharpest that could be found in the time allowed. She caught the Reverend Mother's eye. Yes, she knew the convent's honour was at stake. It always was when she was in the firing line.

Her interrogator cleared his throat. "We will begin."He had been well briefed by the missionary and had in his brain every shocking detail. The question was, could he bring it out of this demur figure sitting opposite him? Looking at her willing expression, he was confident he could. Even so, success would bring a slight twinge of regret. It would mean the fury of the Church falling on the culprit. He had had his moment of delight, now would come the reckoning. Life was full of ups and downs. He tut tutted to himself. A most unfortunate phrase to use in the circumstances.

He felt Sister Adela's innocent gaze upon him. He could see why she was the number one suspect. Very pretty under such amateurish make up. But he mustn't let his thoughts wander. "Close your eyes," he intoned. "Relax. You are falling into a deep sleep. You are going deeper and deeper."

The young girl had never really believed in her purveyor's art. Yet she had to admit her eyelids were becoming heavy. And her mind more hazy. She dug her secret weapon into her palm. She only just avoided saying 'ouch.' but the effort cleared her brain immediately. Striving to keep her features the same, she repeated the process every time drowsiness threatened.

Satisfied at last that she was ready, Pierre decided to start. He had warned his companions that his language would be explicit. There was no other way to do it. They could move back if they wanted to. Chairs scraped noisily, but if anything, these were moved closer.

"It is a sunny April day," he began. "You are in the garden. You sniff the flowers."

"Daffodils," came the responsive murmur.

"You move to the lawn. There is a man. You tremble with excitement. You huff and puff. You take his hand and sit down."

"I huff and I puff," agreed the figure opposite.

Pierre leaned forward. "Yes? Yes?"

"I huff and puff and blow the doll up. "

"No, no. Never mind the doll. The man, the man."

"My man is Henry."

The hypnotist tried another tack. "You are lying on the lawn. Your companion is beside you. The moment comes." His voice found a new urgency. "You are in a fever. What do you do?"

Sister Adela arose as if in a trance. In one movement she flicked off her shoes. Arms outstretched, she slowly began to pull her habit over her head. Her long legs and shapely thighs came into view. There were anguished cries from the audience. Pierre leapt up and hurriedly snapped his fingers as loudly as he could in front of her face. Her startled eyes opened wide. With a gasp of horror she let her garment drop back. She sank into her seat, covering her head in her hands. The sound of sobbing came from between them. The Mother

225

Superior and Henrietta exchanged dismayed glances. Sister Martina struggled to keep her hands together. Otherwise they would have found themselves busy with a sustained burst of clapping. What a performer! She'd fooled the lot of them. There was nothing else the two investigators could do now. They'd shot their bolt. She gave her handkerchief to the young girl to wipe her tears. And in doing so, whispered her congratulations for a magnificent display. Display? gasped her companion. She'd dropped the pin and was spark out. She really believed she was with -. The Reverend Mother swiftly clapped a hand over her mouth. She took back her damp offering and began mopping her own brow. It had suddenly acquired a lot of perspiration. She thanked her lucky stars no one had noticed their exchanges.

The Mother Superior remained far from satisfied. The investigation might be over, but she still had work to do. The Order had to maintain the highest standards. The nuns were allowed certain things for relaxation but a blow up doll would never be on the list. Especially for playing with in public which she quickly pointed out.

Yet Sister Martina was defiant. To put it bluntly, in most convents it was all girls together and hers was no exception. Sister Adela however was not of that persuasion. So it was only fair to give her something to occupy herself with while the others, if the Mother Superior would excuse the expression, were at it. The listener would not excuse it, but was so stunned by the turn of events, that she found no words to say so. The speaker took advantage of her silence to continue. The young girl had been traumatised by Miss Tobias peeping over the wall to see her showing her affection for Henry. Or rather Henry showing his affection for her. When word of this spread round Hatchett, those with fantasies about nuns claimed to have taken part. Gossip had fed gossip. The convent was accused of being a brothel. It was all hot air. More than enough to fill a dozen Henrys twice the size.

The missionary was thinking feverishly. "Wait a minute," she almost shouted. "What about that constable that was really seduced? He was a reliable witness."

The Reverend Mother could barely keep the contempt from her voice. "Reliable witness? The police are always concocting evidence and altering statements. No, the convent has been dreadfully wronged. It has been a distressing experience for the innocent, but we have kept our faith in God and turned the other cheek".

The Mother Superior winced at the choice of words. How unsubtle could you get? In fact Sister Martina's pious outpourings made her feel sick. If only they were true. Yet she was certain they were not. As was the seething figure beside her.

The Reverend Mother meanwhile was busily winding up the proceedings. Did they want to inspect the doll further? If not, she would let it down. It tended to make Sister Adela restless in its present state. Did they want tea before they departed?There were some delicious scones which could be unearthed quickly from the deep freeze. The pair shook their heads. They had lost their appetites. Sister Martina began whistling a little tune. The sound got on their nerves. Henrietta for the first time in a long while found her faith being tested. Which side was the Lord on? She could not believe the Reverend Mother had been praying harder than her for a favourable result. She wondered if rank had anything to do with it. Her adversary had an exalted position in the Church hierarchy while she was just a missionary. No, He wouldn't take that into account. She did just as much good work. If she hadn't been in company, she would have kicked herself in frustration. She did not believe in reincarnation, but if there was such a thing, she was certain Sister Martina was previously the high priestess of Sodom or Gomorrah. Or more likely, both.

The missionary and the Mother Superior made their way to the front of the building followed at a distance by the dazed Pierre. Their hostess strode beside them to say goodbye. She put the flowers still fresh from the patient's bedroom into the car. They took up most of the back seat. After what had happened, the Mother Superior felt she was getting into a hearse. She shook Henrietta by the hand and wished her luck in Africa. They'd had precious little in Hatchett but she remembered the saying ' what goes around, comes around.' She would be keeping an eagle eye on the convent. She had been taught to look on the bright side. She fingered her still tender throat. At least she was alive. Her youthful assistant squeezed in next to her, wondering what her chances were of getting a blow up doll. Judging by the Mother Superior's face, not very high.

Sybil sat back with her eyes closed for the journey home but her brain would not stop racing. She had to hand it to Sister Martina. A deft piece of footwork. Or so it seemed. She was certain there had been skulduggery. But exactly what? That was the problem. The rubber male had been a masterstroke. Surely it was introduced at the last moment? Yet there was no proof. And now there never would be. The Reverend Mother had weathered the storm. You had to feel sorry for Miss Tobias. Or dear Henrietta as she had come to call her. The bible was full of avenging angels, but those in the modern world had much more of a struggle making good prevail over evil.

A young voice broke into her thoughts. "Can I go

and join their Order?" Sister Claire could not keep her eager tone out of it.

"No, you certainly cannot."

Her companion was crestfallen. "Sister Adela has offered to take me under her wing. She does a lot of community work. She said I'd be excellent at it with my youthful vigour. We mustn't shut ourselves off from the world."

The mother Superior stiffened. "It depends which world, child. There are certain parts which should be left well alone. They are past saving."

"But aren't they the ones we should be reaching out to?"

"There has been quite enough reaching out already," came the terse reply which ended the conversation. The speaker uttered a deep sigh. She shouldn't have brought such an innocent creature with her. Three nights under that roof and she was halfway led astray. Mind you, she had almost wavered herself. All those flowers and serenading. But no, she'd proved her worth. As any Mother Superior would. Always keep your wits about you. That was the motto. Even when you've been half strangled.

She settled down again. God sent these things to try his faithful servants. She had given her all and done her best. So she wouldn't be holding anything against Sister Martina. Not for the moment anyway.

Henrietta walked slowly home. Mavis could see by her anguished expression that something was wrong. She listened sympathetically as her friend recounted the harrowing details. She would have to ring Mr Chambers and tell him their efforts had been wasted. Ironically, if Miss Tobias had kept him on one more day the outcome could have been different. He would certainly have checked the doll's delivery date. and it had arrived barely twenty four hours before. Sister

Martina was so worried she had been waiting for the postman in the road.

The missionary packed her belongings. She would miss the cleaner but otherwise was glad to see the back of the village. She had done her best. Although of course, it was beyond help. There were one or two who deserved saving yet they had been badly led astray by the rest. She, like Sybil, tried to be positive. She listed her achievements. The cars were correctly parked, the smoking club was disbanded and those obscene videos were out of sight. This feeling was swiftly replaced by a sinking one. Tomorrow the double yellow lines would be crowded again, there would be a new lighting up time at the Nag's Head, and Mounting Olive would be back on the counter. She gave a big sigh. Was it all wasted energy?

The Reverend Mother felt she deserved her large brandy. She twirled her glass. She put it down and pinched herself. She could hardly believe it. Against all the odds, the convent's reputation was still intact. Well almost. The Mother Superior could think what she liked. What was needed was proof and she had not found any. The nuns had been real heroines. They had rallied magnificently to the cause and so had the village. And none more so than Ada and Dora. All right, they had done a runner, but who wouldn't in that situation? They deserved a reward. They were both widows. Maybe they would like to share Henry? If not, he could be sold on e-bay. From a different address of course. He had played his part now. One thing was for sure, Sister Adela would not be needing him. She would be far too busy. She had a lot of catching up to do. But there must be an end to frolicking outside. There would be no more special requests. The potting shed was perfectly adequate. Especially with its new mattress. Security had to be tightened. It would need a pair of curtains. There must be no more peering in. From any direction.

There was a knock on the door. Sister Adela entered. She was greeted with a dazzling smile. "We have seen off the forces sent against us," said the Reverend Mother who felt like Henry V after Agincourt. Which gave her an idea. "Why did you call it Henry?"

"After my uncle. He was always very keen to bounce me on his knee."

"Well, it certainly did a good job. Miss Tobias couldn't believe her ears. But it was a near thing." She took a sip of brandy, forgetting the young girl was there. "The pimple was on the wrong side. When I ordered it, I forgot to stipulate whether left or right."

Her listener frowned. "What if she thinks about it afterwards? She might come back."

"It will be too late. It's deflated and well hidden. Ready for resale."

Sister Adela sighed. "Maybe we could get a female one. It could stand in for me sometimes."

The Reverend Mother patted her on the knee. "Come now child, you know you enjoy your work and it's for such a good cause. We really do have a hefty bank balance. We will have to decide soon what to spend it on. I was thinking of a share in a race horse."

The young girl did not want to add jockeys and trainers to her list. "Couldn't we go to Lourdes after all? We were so looking forward to it."

Sister Martina put a pensive finger to her lips. "I don't see why not. After all, we have just witnessed a miracle. Not an impressive one by biblical standards, but certainly for Hatchett's." She took another sip and sensed she was being stared at. "It's medicinal. it's for my nerves." She felt a sudden wave of compassion." But yours have been shattered too, haven't they?" She took another glass from a drawer and poured a generous amount into it. She raised her own. "To our saviour."

Sister Adela didn't know whether she meant the Lord or Henry but either would do. She took a tentative gulp. Then another. The aroma was familiar. Where had she smelt it before? Oh yes, on the lawn. That client had breathed it all over her. No wonder he'd been impatient. When she thought about it, he'd had a nerve. The alcohol was coursing through her veins. She suppressed a giggle. She proposed her own toast. "To bottoms everywhere."

Chapter 46

Donald Chambers sat in his armchair clutching a whisky. He had just received Mavis's call and had shaken his head in deep sorrow. Knitting and sewing clubs indeed. He didn't believe a word of it. Those initials stood for real people although at times he felt the whole affair was unreal. So his burglary had been in vain, but what could he do now? Henrietta and that Mother Superior had swallowed a preposterous explanation. Or at least been unable to prove otherwise. And he had to concede there was little else they could have done. He knew better than most that you had to have proof. It could be staring you in the face only you couldn't see it. At other times it remained deeply hidden. He felt this one was not far below the surface.

He helped himself to another largish tot. Had he earned his money? He felt he had. Every last penny. Never mind rescuing Miss Tobias from a coffin. He'd given her the vital information. It was not his fault if she hadn't been able to act on it. And he had fronted up to Bambini. Hardly every day work for a detective. He gave a short laugh. And that blow up doll. You had to admire the Reverend Mother. Her audacity took your breath away. Now that he knew Sister Adela's identity he felt he should challenge her himself. Another whisky and he would make a solemn promise to do exactly that. But sadly, the bottle was empty.

Chapter 47

Henrietta finished the last of her packing. She was returning to Africa and this time by boat. It would be a hurried departure but a slow journey. She needed a break and who wouldn't after spending six months in Hatchett? Was it only that long? It seemed more like six years. Appearances could be so deceptive. It had looked the perfect sanctuary in which to recoup her powers. She suppressed an ironic laugh. That place could match any depravity that the worst of her tribe could think up. And dangerous too. It was amazing, but she'd feel safer where she was going.

But what now? She'd start her stretcher bearing school. Roads were replacing jungle trails. Yet there was still a need for them in the deep interior. And that's where she would be. As far away from Hatchett as possible. But as a servant of the Lord, she must show forgiveness. Her dream last night of her great grandfather's Africa was greatly troubling. Sister Martina had been in the pot. Tied up tightly with tree vines. And she, instead of trying to rescue her, had helped pour in the water. Splashing lots of it on the ground in her excitement. And then ignoring the screams, had discussed the best sort of gravy to go with human flesh. And after that, there'd been the dancing round the victim. All those black bottoms and one white one. It was always there, taunting her. She had borrowed a spear and crept up behind it. And then just in time, she had woken up. It was a great relief. For she knew what she would have done and it would have been a terribly unchristian act. Those spears were extremely sharp and pointed. She frowned. Was she becoming like the very people she was trying to save? Had Hatchett had a bigger effect on her than she had on it? It was a good question but that was all in the past. There was no point in trying to answer it. As her forebear had once memorably said of conversions. You win some, you lose some.

She took a small bottle from her pocket and rolled it in her hand. Talking of those ceremonial dances. That had been her problem. She couldn't let go like the natives. She couldn't join in properly and that had kept her apart. God, she'd tried. How she'd tried. She couldn't get the stamping right. She was always worried about thorns. Or get her elbows to co-ordinate. And she lacked fire. The tom toms did nothing for her. They didn't pound in her ears like they should. But now she'd put everybody to shame. Even the witch doctors. She couldn't wait to get her shoes off. She looked at the potion George had given her. LSD. That's what Mavis had said it was. She'd knock that back and then watch out. But it had to be a big clearing. She didn't want to find herself climbing trees and jumping off branches. She knew it made you feel you could fly. She was quite happy to flap her arms on the ground. She would be a sensation. They had several animal dances but not a chicken one. She wondered what feathers to use and what colours. That could wait until she got there. She put the bottle in her suitcase and closed the lid.

Chapter 48

There was much gleeful raising of glasses in the Nag's Head. News of Sister Martina's victory had swiftly swept the village. It had been greeted with joyous cries of relief among Henrietta's lost souls. The favourites among Mrs Gardner's betting list had been the first to arrive. The landlord was doing brisk business. And among the gulping and back slapping, the revellers were quietly thanking their lucky stars for their salvation.

James surveyed the happy throng and called for their attention. "I know most of you are celebrating not being fingered for certain furtive deeds," he began. "But who was the one who started it all? The fresh air fiend? Now is the time to come clean."

"Maybe it was you," declared the vicar. "Trying to throw us off the scent."

"You can think that if you like," he replied gravely. "But I cannot do without my creature comforts. I need a bed. Not a patch of grass."

"What about the colonel?" ventured Arthur. "He's the outdoor type. He's used to facing the elements. Crawling about in bushes and all that."

"I would certainly not be caught in the open," the military figure replied stiffly. "One learns to blend in with the background. And what about you?" he added. "You have a penchant for showing off your bottom in public."

"Only in films. And then only in the comfort of our flat. I don't like draughts when I'm baring all." He looked across at the doctor. "If you ask me, George is also a suspect. He's always advocating fresh air and exercise."

"I give advice, but I'm not one for following it,"

replied the general practitioner. "That early in the summer there would certainly be a chill factor which would put somebody in my condition off from the start. I've never admitted this before, but I keep my long johns on until June."

"What about Ronnie?" asked the landlord turning to the vicar. "Your sermons are always going on about communing with nature."

"I was not referring to the birds and the bees," he replied hotly. "It is despicable to suggest I would stoop so low to commit such an act. Those of my calling have lofty ideals."

"Come off it," said the newsagent. "Vicars are always running off with their parishioners' wives or fondling choir girls. It's a perk of the job."

"If it's that good, I'm surprised you haven't made a video of it."

"Maybe I will. You can be the technical adviser."

"Now, now," interrupted James. "We're not getting anywhere. I notice constable Tompkins is keeping very quiet."

The object of this remark was standing at the back of the crowd. "It's been difficult to get a word in but there's nothing to say. Police officers don't go taking their trousers off in convent gardens. They're there to uphold the law. Not break it. Even the thought of such an event is deeply distressing."

The landlord refilled a line of glasses. "Well, it looks like we'll never discover who it was. All I can do is offer a toast to the mystery man."

There was a chorus of here, heres.

Yet one smile was a little more fixed than the rest. Its owner held his drink a little tighter. His hear, hear was a little more heartfelt. And every time he now saw a blade of grass he shuddered. And what of his dreams? He was repeatedly erecting broken glass and barbed wire along the top of convent walls.

So who is he?

I'm afraid you'll have to ask Sister Adela.

~ The End ~